EQUESTRIAN BROTHERS

Laura McCathie

Contents

E lena Moore has loved horses ever since she sat on her first pony at the age five, and well since then she has let nothing stop her from reaching her goal, to be a top equestrian by the time she is 18. The only problem is, she's already 16 and has only competed in a few top shows. But when the famous, Alan Pierce, approaches her while she is at a show and offers her a chance to ride for them, she jumps at the offer, thinking this will finally be her chance to get to be where she wants to. But there is only one problem, or should I say two? Alan Pierce as two twin boys, who both ride, and are both extremely gorgeous. What will happen? Find out in 'The Pierce Brothers.'

→ Chapter one

X^x

"I can't believe you're going to be riding with THE Pierces this time tomorrow! You lucky bitch!" my best friend, Sarah, squealed as she ran through my bed room door her light green eyes sparkling with excitement. I laughed softly as I placed the pair of white breeches I had in my hands into the almost full suitcase that was open on my bed with clothes almost over flowing the sides. Sarah has been my best friend ever since she had moved to River wood Stables five years ago, where we clicked instantly.

"Hello to you to Sarah!" I laughed, closing my suitcase before zipping it up,

"Yeah, yeah, hi to you too. How did this even happen?!" she laughed, waving her hand at me, brushing off my hello.

"To be honest, I have no idea. It's like a dream, I keep pinching myself! One minute I was walking the course and the next I was being offered a job at Pierce Stables! It's the sort of think that only happens in movies or books" I smiled shaking my head softly,

"Elena, just promise me one thing ok?" Sarah asked, her voice suddenly turning serious,

"Of course! Anything!" I smiled looking down at my best friend,

"Hook up with those two amazing boys, or I will fly to Kentucky and murder you in the night" She smirked, wiggling her eyebrows.

"Sarah!" I groaned, throwing one of my pillows at her, "You are such a slut! Both of them?!"

"Ok, one then! And bring the other one back for me?" she smiled innocently, giving me her famous puppy dog eyes,

"Uh fine! I'll bring you back one,"

"Promise?"

"You are so weird Sarah." I groaned,

"But you'll miss me and my weirdness," she smiled,

"Of course I will, I'm going to miss you so much S," I frowned sitting beside her. "I'll miss you too! But you're going to have two hot, gorgeous guys! You'll be right mate!" she smiled, her Australian accent coming through, "While little Aussie me will be here ALONE while my best friend will be off in Kentucky living the equestrian dream!"

She was right, I would be living the equestrian dream, every equestrian would kill to be able to even have a few hours with the Pierce brothers, and I would be able to hang out with them whenever I wanted. This is the start of a new life, a life of an elite equestrian.

"Earth to E!" Sarah yelled at me, right in my left ear,

"What?" I asked, snapping out of my little world,

"I was talking to you, but you were just staring into space." Sarah stated, rolling her eyes at me,

"Oh, sorry, I'm was just in my own little world. What where you saying?" I sighed, crossing my legs underneath myself.

"Well I was saying, how are you going to take all your horse gear to Kentucky? It's not going to fit into that little thing." She asked, gesturing over at the small suitcase that I had just finished stuffing all my clothes into,

"Well.. Part of the job offer was that I'd get complete new things. New Saddle, new bridle, new everything!" I smiled, falling back onto the bed.

"Holy shit.. Can I just swap lives with you, right here, right now!" Sarah gasped, falling back beside me, "Did I say you are one lucky bitch?"

"Yes. You've only said that about 10 million, billion times." I laughed, staring up at the roof,

"Hey E?" I heard Sarah asked from besides me

"Yeah?"

"Just don't forget me ok? While you are going round winning top shows and hanging out with amazing guys." Sarah smiled weakly over at me,

"Oh S, I could never forget you! You are my best friend, I can be hanging out with them and make new friends, but you'll always be my best friend, Pink Promise." I smiled, holding out my pinky finger, I know pinky promises might be for little kids, but it's always been our thing, ever since we have met.

"Pinky promise, and remember! If you brake a pinky promise you have to give me a 1,000 dollars," She smiled, linking her pink with mine.

"ELENA! Come on! If we don't leave now you'll be late for your flight!" I heard my mum yell up the stairs, this is it. This was it my last few hours of normality, and then my life will be changed forever. I pulled Sarah into a bone crushing hug as we both got up off my bed,

"I'm going to miss you E," Sarah sniffled into my shoulder,

"Me too S, but you'll come visit. Hell you are coming to see me with my parents in a few weeks!" I smiled, wiping a few tears off my cheek,

"ELENA!"

"COMING!" I yelled back to my mum, "I'll see you soon ok?" I smiled as I picked up my carry on and the handle of my suitcase.

→ Chapter two

Bronwyn

xx

———

I sighed as I leaned my head back on my head rest and closed my eyes, 2 hours and 22 minutes and I'll be in the Pierce's barn, I'll be in their house! I'll be living with them for a year and if I'm lucky, a few more years after that. I couldn't believe I had gotten the chance to even get to talk to Alan, let alone be ask to ride for them. It was a dream come true, I opened my eyes again and looked out into the crystal blue sky that has a few puffy white clouds scattered beneath us, 2 minutes down, only 2 hours and 20 minutes to go.

———

"This is your captain speaking, we will be landing in 5 minutes, so if you could put your seats into the upright position and make sure your trays are secured, we will begin our decent." I heard the pilots voice ring around the plane. I smiled and pushed up my tray and secured it into place, finally! This had been the longest flight I have ever had, it didn't help that I kept thinking about everything bad that could happen when I got to the Pierce's barn. I shook my head and ran my fingers through my dark brunette hair, I felt my ears begin to pop as we slowly made our way down to Kentucky's airport. I forced myself to yawn, relieving the pressure on my ears for just a slight moment.

I felt myself lurched slightly forward as the plane hit the tarmac on the airport's runway, I looked out the window and finally saw the emerald green grass that Kentucky was so famous for. I glanced over the other side and saw the airport streaking past us. As the plane slowed down the airport buildings came into focus.

"Welcome to Lexington, Kentucky. It's half past two in the afternoon. It is also a chilly 16 degrees outside with a slight chance of rain. If you could please remain seated until we have made a complete stop. I hope you enjoyed your flight with American Airlines and we hope to see you again." I heard the airhostess's voice come ring around the plane just as the pilots had a few minutes ago.

———

I grabbed a hold of the handle of my suitcase and haled it off of the conveyer belt, god I shouldn't of packed so much of my stuff, my suitcase weighed a ton. I pulled the leather strap of my carryon bag onto my shoulder and started to make my way to the sliding doors that led out to the main lobby of the airport, where apparently I was meant to meet the driver that was meant to pick me up and drive to the Pierce Stables. I took a deep breath as stepped out to the crowd of people that where waiting outside the departure doors, I scanned the crowds of people and my eyes met with a sign that read, Elena

Moore. I looked up at the man holding a sign but stopped dead in my tracks as my eyes met the familiar face that Sarah and I fangirled over many, many times before at horse shows and at school, Ryan Pierce. I saw him searching the stream of people that had begin to come out of the doors. He hadn't seen me, good, I probably looked like a complete freak starring at him with my mouth hanging open. I quickly closed it and gathered myself up before making my way over to him, I cleared my throat as I got beside him,

"Umm, hi, I'm Elena Moore. I-l-m guessing you're here for me?" I tried to say calmly, I couldn't let him think I was a weird, giggly girl who was in love with someone who they hadn't even met in real-life before.

"Shi..oh hi" He laughed as he quickly looked at me, "sorry, I didn't see you there, you snuck up on me,"

God! He was so adorable! How can someone be so adorable, seriously? No, Elena! Stop it,

"Uh, Elena?" I heard his deep voice ask,

"What? Huh? Sorry.. What did you say?" I asked, feeling my cheeks heat up slightly, I mentally slapped myself, Elena get a hold of yourself, you are acting like a teenager drunk on love.

"It's ok, I was just saying that we should get going, it's an hour's drive to the barn." He laughed as he shook his head, his soft brown eyes sparkling with humour.

"Well we better get on the road then!" I smiled, as I grabbed the handle of my suitcase again,

"Leave that, I'll get it" He stated, moving towards me, reaching out to the handle of my suitcase,

"No, no. It's ok, you'll brake your back with this thing." I smiled as I shook my head at him,

"So is that why you are pulling it? I think I'm a bit stronger than you," He chuckled, a small smirk spreading across his face, I couldn't help but roll my eyes.

"Fine, fine. Just don't way I didn't warn you." I scoffed, rolling my eyes again, which caused him to let out a soft laugh.

"I'll keep that in mine Elena. Now come on, let's go." He smiled as he turned around and started to walk towards the exit, I took a deep breath, this is going to be the best year of my life, I think.

→ Chapter three

Well this is awkward.

I glanced over at Ryan for probably about the hundredth time on the hour drive, we hadn't talked since we got in the car, I had tried a few times but it never seem to be able keep going. The silence in the car was full of awkwardness, I sighed softly as I looked out the window once again, more emerald green pastures. We had left the suburbs almost half an hour ago and since then there have been pasture after pasture after pasture, so fun to watch. Not.

"So. How was your flight?" he asked, breaking the awkward silence,

"It was good, really long though well it seemed long to me even though it was only 2 hours and 22 min..."

"Elena."

"What?" I asked looking over at him, I noticed the corners of his mouth turned up into a slight smirk,

"You were rambling and didn't take a breath." He chuckled, glancing over at me before flicking on the indicator,

"We're here." He smiled, as he turned the wheel into a long tree lined driveway, I couldn't help but let my mouth drop open, it was even more impressive than it was in pictures. The driveway was gated with a black wrought iron gate that had Pierce written on one side and Stables on the other, reading out Pierce Stables, behind it was two lines of oak trees lining the way towards the multiple barns and house that I could just make out. I looked over at Ryan who was looking at me like an amuse expression on his face,

"What?" I asked looking between the gate and him,

"Nothing. Just your reaction." He chuckled as he pressed a button on the remote, making the gates spring to life and slowly start to open, "You'll get use to it, everyone does," He smiled as he rolled the car through the gates. Row after row we passed pristine paddocks with black wooden fencing, a few horses were still in their paddocks, and each and every one of them had the same coat on. Wow, I never knew it was like this, it was like they had copied each and every horse.

"Never seen anything like this I guess?" he smiled as he glanced over at me and my dreamy expression,

"No.. I haven't there is nothing like this in New York! Well there is but I just board at a small local barn, this is amazing! How did you guess?" I asked, looking over at him,

"It's the same look you gave had when you saw me at the airport." He chuckled shaking his head. He saw me? What!! Now he's going to think I'm a creepy girl that is in love with someone she didn't even know,

"Chill, I'm use to it. I get that look everywhere I go. You aren't the only one who can't resist my charm," He smirked, wiggling his eyebrows at me. Was he serious? I looked over at him and raised my eyebrow,

"Someone thinks they are all that." I scoffed as I rolled my eyes, I turned towards to face the front and watched at the main house came into few. Typical, it was massive, everything here was massive! I un clicked my seat belt as Ryan settled the car to a halt. As I got out of the car, I saw the heavy light brown double front door swing open and a woman about 30 stepped out, her long blonde hair blew in the breeze,

"You must be Elena! I'm Samantha, it's finally good to meet you, I've heard a lot about you from Alan." she smiled as she bounced down the stairs and pulled me into a bone-crushing hug. I couldn't help but let out a little laugh, and hugged her back awkwardly,

"Uh. Hi Samantha, it's nice to meet you too."

"Please! Call me Sam! I hope Ryan wasn't too much trouble, the driver was busy taking Alan to a meeting in town." She smiled as she pulled out of the hug and held me at arm's length,

"I was fine Sam." I heard Ryan's voice behind me, "I'll just take this up to your room, if you want I'll show you it at the same time." He continued as he pushed between me and Sam.

"That would be good" I smiled as I pulled the carryon bag onto my shoulder. I glanced over at Sam's face as I made my way up the steps with Ryan, what did she mean when she said I hope Ryan wasn't too much trouble? Guess I would find out sooner or later probably, I took a deep breath as I took a step into the house, this was it. No going back now.

→ Chapter Four

BEEP. BEEP. BEEEEP.

I let out a sigh as I listened to the sharp beeps of my alarm clock ring around my almost empty room that would be mine for a year.

BEEP.BEEP.BEEEEEP.

"Shut up!" I sighed out loud as I pulled the clock off my bedside table and slapped the top of the alarm, making it silent, I placed the clock back where it belonged and threw the heavy amount of warm blankets off of me, Kentucky sure could get cold during the night. What to wear, what to wear.. I repeated over and over in my head as I walked over to my closet. I could go with charcoal breeches and a light orange polo, or I could go with cream breeches and the same polo. I starred at the two breeches and picked up the charcoal pair. It looks better with the polo anyway. I trudged into the bathroom that was off my bedroom and through my clothes onto the counter and switched on taps, making sure it was the right temperate for me.

──────

"Morning Elena! Want some breakfast?" I heard Samantha call as I passed the kitchen door, I stopped and backed up,

"Morning Samantha, uh, is it ok if I just take an apple? I'm not that hungry." I smiled as I walked in, pointing to a bowl on the counter top full with apples,

"Of course you can! Oh by the way, Alan is waiting for you in the stable office, he needs to go over a few things before you start work." She smiled as she picked and apple and threw it to me,

"Oh ok, thank you! I'll see you later," I nodded as I caught the apple and briskly walked out the door,

"Shit! Boot." I groaned as stepped out of the front door, my socked feet meeting with the damp wooden entrance. I turned around and smack, I walked straight into someone's chest,

"ow.." I groaned as I rubbed my forehead slightly, as I looked up to see who it was and it was none other than Ryan.

"Forget something?" He laughed as he held up my black leather Parlanti tall boots in his hand,

"Why do I always seem to run into you and not your brother, I haven't even met or seen him yet!" I sighed as I took my boots from him, "and how did you even know these where mine?!" I questioned him as I took a seat on a bench that was just beside the front door,

"That's probably because he goes to bed early and gets up 2 hours before you, and well there have never been tall boots that small round here before." He answered as I was zipping up the back of my boots.

"So ready to go?" He asked as I stood up, I took a bite of my apple and looked at him,

"You work in the barns as well?" I asked surprised, my eyebrows raising slightly,

"Don't look so surprised would you? My dad makes me work just as hard as any of you riders." He joked, taking my apple from me before taking a bite,

"OI! Get your own bloody apple Pierce." I frowned as I took it back from him, "any of us rider? Slow down there buddy, some of us riders might be better riders than you," I winked as I took another bite of my apple before starting to walk down the stairs, leaving Ryan standing there with his mouth wide open.

"You coming Pierce?" I yelled not looking round once.

"Of course, someone needs to show you were the stable office is." He laughed as he jogged to catch up with me, that was true.. to be honest I had no idea where I was going, I thought I would just walk to one of the many barns and hope the office was in there.

———

Holy Shit.. That all that I can say and think about their stables, it's like something you can only dream of! Everything was immaculate, no dirt on the hallways what so ever. Each and every horse looks perfect, their manes perfectly pulled, no sign of dirt on them at all and their coats gleaming in the natural light that peaked through the doors that led out to individual yards.

"So, this is the main barn where the Matt and I keep our horses along with the riders, the other barns are for people who board here, I'll show you around later. There are a total of 30 horses in here, 15 to the left and 15 to the right, and five of the will be yours. Dad will tell you who when you go see him in a bit. Oh and the stable office is over there." He smiled, pointing over at a door to our right, I just stared around the place, trying to gather in all the perfection that was this place.

"This is...wow..This place...wow.." I stuttered, I must look like a complete freak but at the moment, I could care less. I just couldn't get my head around all of this! I couldn't get my head around that I was here to be honest, me! A small rider, riding with these big names in the equestrian world. I heard Ryan let out a small chuckle,

"What?" I said, snapping out of my day dream,

"Just your face, you look like a little kid on Christmas." He smirked, god, how can he make a smirk look so freaking amazing. I usually hate it when guys smirk but gah! He was just so perfect. I wonder if his brother was the same as him.

"Shut it Pierce!" I laughed, nudging him slightly,

"Whatever Moore, I will see you later for that tour arena the place." He laughed before giving me a wink and walking down the right side of the barn. I couldn't help but let a small smile creep onto my face, he was just what I thought he would be, charming and perfect.

"You don't think you actually have a chance with him do you?" I heard someone scoff from behind me, I turned quickly around to see a blonde girl, with blue eyes death starring me,

"Pardon?" I asked, raising my eyebrows at her,

"Are you deaf or something? I said, you don't think you actually have a chance with Ryan Peirce do you? What are you a groom? Ryan doesn't date grooms." She laughed, walking closer to me, her arms crossed,

"I heard what you said, and I don't even know what you are talking about. I was just talking to him," I replied, crossing my arms as well, who was this girl? Whoever she is, she's a bitch.

"Oh please, shut it Pierce" She mimicked, throwing her arms in the air, "You were full on flirting with him. Well back off, because he's mine. Not yours. Mine." She spat, walking even closer to me.

"Leave her alone Rebecca." I heard another voice from behind me, Rebecca? So that was her name,

"What are you talking about? I was just welcoming her to the barn," She laughed, plastering a fake smile on her face, "I'll see you around," she smiled before pushing past me and walking down where Ryan has disappeared too, I turned around to see a girl about my height and age standing in front of me,

"Ignore her, she's the Barn Bitch." the girl smiled, "I'm Amelia. But you can call me Amy. Everyone does, my dad sent me too look for you and well, here you are, I didn't have to look very far!" She smiled, shaking her head slightly,

"Your dad? You're Ryan and Matt's sister?" I asked cocking my head to the side,

"Yeah, that's me! Ryan and Matts little sister," she smiled, "now come on, he's waiting in the indoor arena for you."

"I thought it was the stable office." I asked pointing to the door next to myself,

"Oh yeah it was, but he wants to see how you go on one of your horses you've been given, come on, I'll show you the way," She smiled, before pulling me towards the exit.

I was already getting the chance to ride? I thought I'd have to do a few things before he even let me touch a horse of my own! I took a deep breath, this is the time to impress him. No messing up. I have to do everything perfect. I looked down the hallway that Ryan and that Rebecca girl went down and saw them down talking to each other, who was she to tell me I better stay away from him? It's not like she was his girlfriend, or was she?

→ Chapter five

_____

___ "Elena! So good to see you again!" I heard a deep, booming voice erupt around me as I entered the indoor arena, where two males where standing smack dab in the middle of the arena, one of them being the one that sent his booming voice across at me, the other one looked familiar but I couldn't see from the entrance and they had with them a beautiful dapple grey. It looked like the horse I dreamed about every since I was a little girl, I think this horse is pretty much every equestrians dream horse to be honest.

"I'll see you later ok? I have to go to a few things, hope your first day goes well!" Amelia smiled before turning on her heels and walking away back towards the stables. I put on a big smile as I reached the middle of the arena and looked at the older man, who I know as Alan Pierce.

"It's good to see you again sir," I smiled again, giving the hand he held out towards me a strong shake. You can always tell what the person is like by what their hand shake is like, well at least that is what my step-dad told me.

"Oh please, call me Alan. None of this sir business! Anyway I know you have met Ryan, so this is Matt. Matt this is Elena, our new rider." He smiled, as he pointed at his son and then me, and then back at Matt. I looked up at him and smiled, he wasn't as good looking as his brother, don't get me wrong he is freaking hot and would give any guy back home I know competition but he just didn't have the same look as his brother. Unlike his brother he had softer features and was more neater looking, his hair didn't look like he had just woken up, it look sort of brushed, I guess and he looked younger than Ryan, even though they were twins. I could tell, Matt was nothing like Ryan at all.

"Hey, it's nice to meet you," he smiled, offering his hand towards me like his father, which I took gladly,

"It's nice to meet you too," I smiled back,

"Ok so! You are probably wondering who this horse here is huh? Of course you are!" he continued, not giving me any time to respond, "this is your main horse, Maddie. She's a 16.3 hand, 6 year old, Dutch Warmblood, and she's the best horse I have seen for a while. I would of given her to either Ryan or Matt but they have five horses going each at the moment, so I chose to give her to you. But be warned, she's not the easiest ride. So Matt, get on up there and show Elena what she's in for, I'll go and get that double set," he smiled, before jogging away towards a double that was at the far corner of the arena, I could feel knots in my stomach starting to form which were quickly joined by a few butterflies, she couldn't be that hard could she? He wouldn't put me on a horse that he knew I might not be able to handle?

"Relax, my dad's is making her sound harder than she is. She's actually a sweetheart" Matt smiled, looking down at me. I snapped my neck up towards him, god, why are they both so tall, they were probably about 6 foot, maybe even taller? I guess my shortness didn't help, since I was only 5'3.

"What? I'm not worried." I lied, plastering a smile onto my face, hiding the nervousness that should be showing.

"Really? Is that why you looked like you were going to throw up anytime soon? he chuckled before getting placing his foot into the stirrup, swinging himself into his Antares saddle. I have always wanted one of those saddles... Well I want everything on that horse. Including the person. Ok that was uncalled for, shut up Elena! I let out a nervous laugh and slapped my hand over my mouth, hoping he didn't hear that.

"Sorry, I heard that." He winked, before he urged Maddie into what looked like a floating trot. Her movements where gorgeous, well all of her looked gorgeous! She was soft and supple, working beautifully from behind and she bounced with every step. Her movements are what equestrians only dream about, and she's mine! Nothing could spoil this, I could feel my confidence growing as I watched Matt turn Maddie to the a simple 4 foot vertical, which she popped over like it was only a pole on the ground. Wow, I knew Matt was a good rider, well better than good more like an amazing rider, but he made everything look effortless. I couldn't even see any aids being used from him, it was like he was controlling Maddie telepathically. After a few more jumps, Matt halted in front of me,

"Ready?" He smiled before swinging himself off and walked towards me, I nodded, wait.. my helmet!

"Damn it! I forgot my helmet!" I grumbled, looking at him,

"No worries, just borrow mine," he laughed, before removing it off of his head, before placing it on mine, ok. This might be a stupid thing to fan girl over, but I am wearing Matt Pierce's helmet! Suck it bitches back home that didn't really believe I was coming here. Boy would they be jealous.

"Thanks," I smiled, before taking the reins from his hand and throwing them over Maddie's ears. I took a deep breath as Matt threw me effortlessly onto her back. I gathered the reins in my hands and pressed softly with my calves which made her erupt like a spring into her trot. Wow, this has got to be the most amazing trot, wait, amazing horse I have ever sat on.

———

So far so good, all her movements where a dream to ride to. Her walk was energetic but controllable, her trot was springy but easy to sit to and her canter, don't even get me started, it's probably one of the most smoothest, rocking horse canters to sit to ever! Ok so maybe everything was a bit better than so good. More like amazing.

"Matt! Will you chuck that vertical down to about 3'5. Just for Elena's first jump on her," I heard Alan call over to Matt who was leaning on the rising oxer that was the last jump in the double, just silently watching me ride.

"sure thing." He replied, pushing on the jump and making his way over to it before adjusting it to the right height,

"Now Elena, come round at a steady canter a pop that. That's easy for her she's jumping much, much higher." I nodded as I pushed Maddie into her rocking canter.

I took a deep breath as I rounded the corner, 4 exact strides to the jump, this should be easy. I thought to myself, as I gathered her up underneath me, remembering Alan said to keep her steady before the jump. I felt her immediately gather up and stead herself under me, god this horse was perfect, I could already tell she would take me far. 1 more stride. I felt her take of under me, pushing off and clearing it with easy. I closed, making sure to keep my position perfect. My eq was one of my strongest points. As we landed on the ground I couldn't help but let a huge grin come over me.

"She's amazing!" I smiled, giving her a large pat on the neck.

"You think that's amazing? Try her higher! Matt put it up to 4' and can I say, you have perfect eq. Don't you think Matt?" Alan praised, giving me a nod,

"One of the best I've seen in a while to be honest." Matt laughed, putting the rail back into the cup. Did that really just happen? Did both Alan and Matt Peirce say I had amazing eq? This day couldn't get any better! I smiled as I pushed Maddie into her canter again, before lining up the vertical that was set at its new height.

→ Chapter six

_____

___ "You didn't tell me you where such an amazing rider." I heard a familiar voice say from behind me. I glanced over my shoulder as I ran the soft brush over Maddie's dappled coat.

"Thanks Matt. That means a lot coming from you." I smiled as continued to run the brush down Maddie's already soft, clean coat.

"You know you don't have to brush her. We have grooms for that." He laughed leaning against the wooden wall in front of where Maddie was cross-tied.

"Well. I haven't been use to grooms, I've always done everything myself, brushed, washed, clean tack. I did everything, plus I love spending time with horses. I love doing all that stuff, it's a part of the sport." I laughed,

"I guess I'm the opposite, I've always had everything done for me, god that makes me sound so stuck up," he sighed, running his fingers through his hair, I glanced over at him and looked straight into his brown, mahoganny eyes,

"You have never done anything for yourself?" I questioned, raising my eyebrows at him, he can't be serious, he must of at least brushed a horse!

"Don't make me feel even worse than I am. I did when I was younger, I just don't have time for it anymore." He sighed, looking straight back into my almost black ones.

"Well you should make time, how else are you going to bond with your horse? But I see where you are coming from. Being a big hot shot in the equestrian world can take its toll. Well at least it looks like it does." I smiled, before breaking the eye contact we kept for a while, his eyes where softer than Ryan's, Matt seemed to be the more caring one.

"I know I shou.." but before he continued his sentence he was cut off,

"Well I've seen you've met each other" Ryan smirked before patting his brother on the shoulder,

"I saw you riding Elena, you where beast," He continued. I glanced over at Matt who was staring at Ryan, the softness in his eyes had been replaced with a death stare, what was that about? I don't think Ryan had noticed it, because his eyes were glued on me,

"Thanks. But I wasn't.. uh.. beast. I was ok." I laughed unsurely, raising my eyebrows slightly.

"Ignore him he's trying to be cool. Which isn't working." Matt scoffed, looking over at Ryan,

"Someone is on their period today." Ryan scoffed back raising his eyebrows at his brother. Wow.. boys could be such jerks. An uncomfortable silence fell as Ryan and Matt death stared each other,

"Well..uh..I'm just going to go and put Mads back in her stall why you two kill each other with your eyes. I'll see you around." I laughed, and before they could say anything I unclipping Maddie from the cross-ties and started walking her towards her new stall.

I pulled open the bolt and swung the door open and led Maddie in before closing the door behind me, making sure I secured the top and bottom bolt. I smiled softly as I watched Maddie wonder over to her hay net and start munching it contently.

"Do you know why Ryan and Matt are bitchy at each other?" I heard someone laugh as they lent against Maddie's stable door, I glanced over and saw Amelia, I laughed and shook my head,

"I have no idea. Matt was just talking to me and then Ryan came and then they just started to death stare each other." I laughed again, placing Maddie's brown leather halter on the hook outside her stable.

"Oh! That makes sense now." She smiled,

"What makes sense?" I asked raising my eyebrows up at her, I hated when someone said that, I always want to know more!

"She's a beautiful horse, you are so lucky!" She laughed, trying hard to switch the subject,

"Amelia. Don't change the subject, what makes sense?!" I huffed, putting my hands on my hips, she looked at me a groaned slightly,

"Fine! Don't you see? They both like you." She sighed, rolling her eyes at me,

"I've only been here for a day! How can they like me already!?" I gasped, they liked me? How, why? Neither of them can like me, it's impossible. Amelia just has the wrong end of the stick, they probably hate me and are just trying to be nice to me, and they are actually talking about how much they hate me right now.

"They have seen you around a bit, but don't worry Ryan has a girlfriend and Matt... Well Matt is single." She laughed patting me on the shoulder, "I got to go ride my horse Sully. I'll see you at home tonight," she smiled before turning on her heels and skipping off down the aisle.

"AMELIA!" I shouted after her which caused everyone to turn around but her. I groaned as I looked back at Maddie,

"They can't like me. I've only been here for a day and I doubt they've seen me out.. I've only been to a few shows they've been at, and I've been in the smaller classes. Amelia is wrong, isn't she Mads?" I wondered out loud to Maddie, I smiled softly as she gave me a small, soft nicker, nodding her head slightly,

"That's what I thought too.." I smiled. But a little part of me hoped that Amelia was right..

→ Chapter seven

___

___ I groaned in frustration as I walked down the same aisle for about the 100th time, why did think place have to be so bloody massive! All I wanted to do was go to the feed room and get Maddie a carrot, but no. I had to be stuck walking around this stupid place, ok maybe I was happy to be lost for the first few minutes, I got to look around the place more. But after a while it wore off. I just wanted a stupid carrot!

"You lost?" A deep, familiar voice laughed, I jumped slightly and put my hand on my forehead,

"Ryan!" I screeched, looking at his smirking face behind the black steel bars of the stable, he was in with a gorgeous bay, who had a blaze that covered most of his face and upper lip.

"So, are you lost?" he repeated, and from what I could tell he was trying his hardest not to laugh,

"I..am not lost." I lied, walking over to the stable door and patting the bay on his soft muzzle "Who's this?" I smiled, trying to veer him away for me being lost,

"His name is Caesar, and he happens to be another one of your horses, so, if you are lost, why are you wondering round with that look on your face?" he laughed, patting Riot on his neck.

"He's one of mine?" I gasp, un-bolting the stable and letting myself in, "he's gorgeous!" I smiled, running my hand down Caesar's solid, muscular neck. I felt my hand softly brush over Ryan's, I looked up at him, my brown eyes locking with his own. I studied his eyes, which were staring intently into my own, I saw a hint of softness cross them. He looked even more gorgeous than before, how can that hint of softness in his eyes make him even more attractive? How is that even possible? I quickly snapped out of the gaze we had and quickly pulled my hand away. I quickly ducked under Caesar's neck as I felt my cheeks heat up, I hoped to god Ryan didn't see, it would make his ego even bigger than it already was.

"Well..u..uh." Ryan stuttered, is he lost for words? I glanced over Caesars back at him, he was looking over at me, I quickly composed myself and looked over at him,

"Can you tell me where the feed room is? I just want a freaking carrot for Mads and well now Caesar as well." I asked biting my bottom lip softly.

"You walk out of the barn and then turn left and there is an add on to the barn and that is the feed room and you'll find carrots in the fridge, so I was right, you where lost!" he laughed, pointing his finger at me,

"Yes. I was lost. You were right. Now I'm going to go get my carrots. I'll see you later baby!" I smiled as I kissed Caesar on the nose and let myself out of the stable, quickly closing it behind me and walking swiftly down the aisle.

"See you later babe!" I heard Ryan shout behind me, I looked over my shoulder and saw him smirking at me,

"You're a jerk, you know?!" I shouted at him as I rounded the corner, making my way out of the barn and into the feed room. I finally let a smile cross my face as I leant against the wall of the feed room,

"What the hell just happened?" I wondered out loud as I let my head lean back against the wall, I breathed in deeply again and let it out as I crossed the room to the fridge and reached in and grabbed a few carrots, one for Caesar, one for Maddie and one for myself.

———

I sighed in relief as I finally threw myself down onto my soft, comfy bed. As much as I loved working with horses it sure was good to finally be back in bed.

Knock, knock, knock.

I groaned as I rolled off my bed and dragged myself over to the door and throwing it open, I groaned again as I saw Ryan leaning against my door frame.

"What do you want?" I sighed, looking up at him and raising my eyebrows,

"Nice to see you too Elena," he smirked,

"Hi, now please go away I want to sleep." I sighed, trying to pushing him back so I could close my bedroom door, but he didn't move a budge.

"What are you made of? Freaking steel?" I scoffed, rolling my eyes, trying to push him once again.

"You may as well stop pushing, I'm not moving." he laughed, wiggling his eyebrows,

"Whatever, stand there all night, I don't care!" I scoffed, dragging my feet over to my bed again, I let myself fall onto it face first,

"So I take it you don't want anything to eat?" He asked,

"Food?!" I yelled, before pushing myself off the bed and rushing over to him, but as I reached him he lifted the plate out of my reach,

"Ryan!" I groaned as I crossed my arms over my chest,

"One condition, after you eat this, I take you to look around the place." He smiled, looking down at me,

"I am not looking around this place as.." I glanced over at the clock and then looked back at him "9 o'clock at night!"

"Fine then, no food." He smiled, before turning around, I felt my stomach grumble as he started walking down the hall. Damn you stomach, why do you need food?!

"Fine, FINE! I'll let you show me around. Now give me the freaking burger!" I wined, stepping out into the hall, he turned around and held out the plate to me,

"Now was that so hard?" he smiled, I let out a small laugh and shook my head which made his smile fade quickly,

"Sucker." I yelled before slamming the door and locking it,

"Elena! Really?!" He yelled at me through the door,

"You shouldn't get in the way of a girl and her food! It'll come and bite you in the ass Peirce." I yelled back at him, I heard him let out a frustrated sigh as I took a bite of my burger, so worth what I was probably going to get tomorrow as pay back.

→ Chapter eight

___

___ "UP, UP, UP! IT'S A NEW DAY!" I heard someone scream into my ear, my eyes flew open with shock and my eyes met with the familiar brown ones of Ryan, he was leaning over me with a smirk on his face, I groaned and rolled onto my back pulling a pillow over my head, so this was his pay back? Yelling in my ear to wake me up? Wow, I thought he could do better than that.

"Leave me alone," I crocked sleepily into my pillow,

"No thanks." He stated, I could tell from his voice that he was still smirking, I felt the bed dip down from his weight,

"Get off!" I grumbled, kicking him with my feet. I let out a groan as he ripped the pillow out of my hands, "Fine! I'm up, how will you get out and let me wake up 100 percent?" I continued, letting out a sigh as I sat up,

"I have the perfect thing to wake you up though." He smirked, looking at me,

"And what woul... RYAN!" I screamed as he poured a whole glass of water over me, the freezing water hitting me like ice, "Get out of my fucking room!" I yelled as I smacked him in the face with my pillow again and again,

"Ok! Ok! I'm going" he chuckled, "At least it worked. You're awake." he continued, a smirk plastered over his face,

"Get out jerk!" I sighed, throwing my pillow at him again as he made his way out of my room, god! He was so freaking annoying, I hate him, even if I have been here for a day he was already like my annoying big brother. I guess I did deserve it for last night, but still, bloody jerk. I looked over at my clock and groaned, 4:28am, I didn't even have to get up for another two hours. I'm going to kill him. I threw the covers off of me and pulled open my door Ryan had shut behind him and stormed off down the hall, I stopped in front of the door I thought was his room and took a deep breath as I pulled it open,

"Ryan! You fuck.. OH MY GOD!" I screamed as I covered my eyes and turned around, "I'm so sorry!" I exclaimed, this was not Ryan's room. This was the freaking bathroom, one that was currently being used by Matt. I heard him let out a chuckle,

"I'm sorry! I thought this was Ryan's room, he said it was the third door on the left." I exclaimed, "I'll just leave now.. and let you ah, get dressed." I stuttered, walking out the door and closing it behind me before hurrying back to my room. God, I don't think I'll ever, ever face Matt again after I saw. Ok I'm not even going to talk about it! I groaned and throw myself onto my bed and pulled my covers over myself, I am never, ever coming out of here again.

———

I peeked around the corner making sure the tack room was clear, after see it was clear of both Pierce brothers, I slipped in and grabbed the last thing I needed before giving Maddie a ride, my Antares saddle. I took it in both my arms and stepped out and bang, I walked straight into someone,

"I'm sorry!' I laughed, backing up slightly,

"That's the second time today you've said sorry to me," I heard the person in front of me chuckle, I glanced up and my eyes widened in shock, just the person I had been avoiding all day which I had successfully done up till now,

"I..uh." I stuttered, my mind going complete blank, all it did was go back to this morning in the bathroom, I felt my cheeks heat up slightly but I took a deep breath, trying to keep the embarrassment showing in my face, I pushed everything I was feeling and put a smile on my face,

"Hi." I smiled "uh, sorry about this morning." I continued, shifting my saddle slightly in my arms.

"Well, if you hadn't had run out of the bathroom, you would of let me say that it's fine," he laughed,

"It might of been fine for you but for me it was awkward as hell, that bloody jerk of a brother you had gave me the freaking wro.."

"Elena." he laughed interrupting my rambling

"Yeah?" I nervously asked, looking up at him

"Will you stop rambling. It's seriously fine." He laughed, "Now give me that saddle, you look like your arms are going to fall off at any moment.

"I'm fine.." I laughed, feeling a little bit better than I did this morning after walking in on him,

"Ok, well, my dad just asked me to find you and tell you to hurry up because your lesson starts in 2 minutes,"

"Shit! Are you serious? I thought it was at 3." I cursed, stepping round Matt before starting to walk down the aisle,

"Well... it's 2:59 now, so you really have only 1 minute left, I'll help you get ready." he stated as he caught up with me,

"You, Matthew Pierce, are a life saver!" I smiled as we rounded the corner.

→ Chapter nine

September the 27th - 2 weeks later

"Elena! Close from your hips! You're just throwing yourself over the jumps," Alan yelled at me as I did another failed attempt at getting my eq perfect over a 4'9 vertical.

"What is up with you today? I saw you jump this perfectly yesterday!" he continued shaking his head slightly, I let out a frustrated sigh,

"Come here," he said as we waved me over with his hand, oh god. Please don't let him do what I think he's going to do! I don't think I'll survive it being as tired as I am. I had worked non-stop today from 6 till 3 and I've been up since about, and I had half an hour of full on flatwork, getting my flying changes and transitions almost perfect. Yes Maddie has already got them down packed but me? Apparently I needed to sit better to everything so that was that. I let out a groan as Alan walked to my side and gestured for me to move my leg, letting him get to the stirrups. In one fluid motion he took them off, fuck, he was doing what I didn't want him to do. No stirrups, every riders worst nightmare. Yes it did make you have a stronger leg and give you better eq in the long run, but doing in the short run? It was torture. Alan gave a small chuckle as he placed my stirrups leathers and irons beside him,

"Now. Go do the vertical again," he smiled, pointing at me and then the jump. I let out a sign and pressed my spurs softly into Maddie's side urging her into her smooth, rocking horse canter. God, I loved this horses movements she made everything so easy to sit to without stirrups while some other horses bounced you everywhere.

As I rounded the corner to the vertical I took a deep breath and let it out slowly, trying my best to calm the nerves slightly that had started to bubble up in my stomach, I have never jumped this high without stirrups, ever, the highest I had jumped was about a 3'9 vertical. I felt Maddie quicken her pace underneath me which resulted in me giving her a soft half-halt, which just checked her on her speed. I pushed my heels down and put my calves on and felt Maddie take off, shit, long spot. I felt her leap forward unseating me completely.

"Shit!" I squealed as we launched into the air, I felt myself slipping from the saddle, but it was too late to hold onto her neck, I hit the ground, hard. I landing right on my back and felt the air get knocked right out of me. I tried to take deep breaths as I heard footsteps running towards me, I guess I should of moved, I probably freaked them all out. I felt myself getting my breath back and I closed my eyes, urging myself to take long, deep breaths.

"Elena?!" I heard a familiar voice ask urgently as he put his hand on my shoulder, I felt shivers run down my spine from his touch,

"You should know not to touch a person who has just fallen off," I said, opening my eyes to see Matt's concerned face hovering over mine, but was taken over by relief and his mouth broke into a smile, I groaned as I tried to sit up but Matt softly pushed back down to the ground,

"And, you should know better than to stay still until we know you are ok," he stated,

"I'm fine!" I laughed, pushing his hand away from me as I sat up, I looked up at him, my eyes locking with his own, I gave him a reassuring smile,

"Well at least let me help you up," he sighed as he stood up and held his hand out to me, I looked up at him again and hesitated slightly before reaching up to grab his hand. I sucked in air through my teeth and pain rushed down my left leg,

"You ok?" Matt asked, looking at me, concern all over his face once again, I nodded slightly and took a step forward but pain shot through my leg once again,

"Yes." I said through gritted teeth as I tried to put weight on my leg again, I jumped slightly as I felt Matt loop his arm around my waist, I looked at him quickly and raised my eyebrows,

"No you aren't, don't lie. I saw your face when you put weight on your left leg. Don't look at me like that, I'm helping you walk" He chuckled as he pulled me closer into his side, so I wouldn't have to put any weight on my left leg, I couldn't help but squeal inside, A Pierce's arm is around my waist! Really Elena? You're thinking that now, you just had quite a big fall and all you can think about it a Pierce's arm around your waist? I mentally kicked myself forever thinking about that!

"tha..Wait! Where's Maddie?" I asked urgently, looking around the indoor, where I could see no sign of Maddie,

"She's over there you dork." Matt laughed as he point towards the entrance where Amelia was holding Maddie, she looked good, a bit frightened but fine, I let out a sigh of relief. I don't know what I'd do if something happened to her.

"Why is she up!" I heard Alan shout at us as he walked into the indoor quickly followed by a woman who was holding a first-aid kit,

"I'm fine. No need for that." I lied, putting on a smile,

"She's not ok, she's lying. She can hardly walk." Matt said, I could feel him glaring at me, but I kept looking straight at Alan,

"I said I'm fine. Can I just get back on and do it again, please?!" I huffed, just because my leg is a bit sore, ok maybe it was more than a bit sore, it was agony, but I can't let that stop me! I needed to do it again to prove it to myself and them that I could do it.

"If you let Sophie here check you out and if she gives you the all clear, I will let you do it again." Alan sighed, something told me he knew I wouldn't give just leave it for the day, I was dedicated. Nothing stops me from riding. I thought for a moment and finally nodded, Matt helped me over to the viewing-box and set me down on a seat as Sophie came in first-aid kit in tow.

"I'm just going to take your boot off and roll up your breeches ok?" Sophie explained as she grabbed the zip of my tall boots and pulled, I took a sharp breath as pain once again shot up my leg.

"That hurt?" Sophie asked as she placed the boot beside her, I nodded in return, I felt a few tears gather up in my eyes as the pain continued to throb and shot up my leg, it felt better when my boot was on!

"Ok so this might hurt again, ok? Someone give me something to let her squeeze where I take of her socks and roll up her breeches." She asked, looking around at Alan who was standing next to her and Matt who was kneeling down beside me, I felt Matt pick up my hand and put it in his own,

"I'm not squeezing you hand. I'll kill yo..OW!" I yelled at Sophie yanked off my sock and pushed up my breeches in one quick moment, I raised my eye brow at her

"Sorry, I thought I'd do it when you where distracted," she muttered as she studied my now swollen ankle. I looked at her intently as she finally looked up, but she avoided my eyes and looked at Alan and slowly shook her head who nodded in return,

"Sorry Elena. But you're not riding anytime soon," he sighed, running his hand throw his short brown hair, what? What does he mean I won't be riding anytime soon?

"Can someone please tell me, why I can't ride anytime soon?" I asked, my voice filled with annoyance,

"Your ankle is very badly sprained, I'd say that you've done almost everything in it," Sophie explained her eyes soft,

"But I landed on my back. How can it have happened?" I asked surprised, I looked around at everyone, Matt was looking down at our hands that where still entwined, I slowly pulled my hand out of his and I could feel a soft blush on my cheeks but I tried to ignore it.

"I'm guessing you landed on your ankle and then fel..."

"How long am I not allowed to ride for?" I interrupted, looking her dead in the eye, I saw her mouth open but before she spoke she let out a soft sigh,

"I'd say you'd be lucky to be walking in a week."

———

OH NO :O

→ Chapter ten

You'd be lucky to be walking in a week. Those where the words that kept running non-stop through my head since this afternoon. This couldn't be happening, I've only been here for a few weeks, I can't just stop riding for god knows how long. I let out a groan as I pushed myself off of the bed Matt helped me up to a few hours ago, I hadn't moved since then so I was still in my dirty riding clothes. I braced myself for a wave of pain to sweep up my leg as I softly placed my right foot on the ground,

"1..2..3!" I said out loud to myself, egging myself on. I stood up on 3 and lightly placed the ball of my foot on the ground. I slowly hobbled my way over to my closet and pulled open the sliding doors. I sighed as I pulled out my favourite pair of jeans, a comfy grey sweater and my uggs.

I turned on the shower and held my hand under it making sure it was the right temperature before I ridden myself of my sweaty, dusty riding clothes before stepping into the steaming shower, letting the warm water rush over myself.

———

I sighed softly as I grabbed my soft, cuddly horse pillow pet and made my way to my bed room door, as I pulled it open I stopped dead when I saw Matt blocking the way,

"I was just coming to see how you are doing. Where are you going?" He asked, raising his eyebrows at me,

"Downstairs to watch TV. What else? It's not like I can ride," I sighed pulling my pillow pet closer to my chest,

"What is that thing?" He laughed, flicking it's ear,

"It's not a thing! His name is Sully and he's my pillow pet," I explained holding onto it tighter, it was the only thing I had of my father.

"Ok then.. You know there is a tv in your room right?" He chuckled, putting his arm around my shoulder as he turned me around, ushering me back to my bed,

"No.. Where is it?" I sighed, looking around my room as I fell back down onto the bed, I guess I wasn't getting out of this room for a while,

"Right here." He smiled, pressing a button on a remote that he pulled out of my bed side table and a flat screen tv started to rise from the cabinet opposite my bed,

"Rich people and their gadgets," I sighed, shaking my head, I shuffled back on my bed and leant against my bed head. I took the remote that Matt held out to me and I began switching from channel to channel figuring out what I wanted to watch. I felt the bed sink down as Matt lay down on the bed next to me. In the past few weeks, Matt and I have gotten surprisingly close, while Ryan was like my overly-protective big brother, Matt was more of my best friend. I glanced over at him and raised my eyebrows,

"And what are you doing?"

"Isn't it obvious? I'm watching tv."

"Matt. Get out, I want to be by myself."

"Nope. Sorry. No can do."

I glared at him and punched him in the arm, he could be a real pain in the butt sometimes. Didn't he see I wasn't in any mood to hang out.

"Geeze Elena, don't break my arm," he smiled, rubbing his arm where I had punched him,

"Then you'll know how I feel!" I sighed pulling Sully up over my head, I could feel a few tears prickingly my eyes and I was not going to let Matt see me cry. I heard him let out a long sigh before he pried Sully away from my face,

"Elena..." he sighed, staring right into my eyes.

"What?" I huffed, trying my hardest not to let the tears that had gathered in my eyes out

"Are you ok?" He asked, concern filling his voice,

"Oh yes. I am 100% fine, thanks for asking," I scoffed, what the hell was he doing? Of course I wasn't fine, I just found out I wouldn't be able to ride for god knows how long and it was killing me already!

"Ok, that was a stupid thing to ask."

"Oh no really?"

We fell into an awkward silence as I continued to flick through the channels, finally settling on re-runs of friends. I heard Matt clear his throat but I didn't look at him, I kept my eyes glued on the tv,

"Sophie said you could probably ride in a few weeks.." he said,

"That's not going to help me," I whispered back, barely loud enough for him to hear me, to be honest I'm surprised he even heard me at all,

"What do you mean?" he asked, putting his hands on my hips before turning me towards him, damn it why did he have to do that? I stared at my hand not wanting to look up at him.

"You've forgotten haven't you." I sighed, closing my eyes hard, blinking away the tears that where blurring my vision,

"Forgotten what?"

"It's my first major competition on Maddie next weekend and I'm going to miss it. Because of this stupid fucking accident!" I sighed as I finally looked up at him,

"Oh shit.. Elena, I'm sorry" he sighed, pulling me into one of his hugs that I loved. I felt so secure and safe in his arms, it's like I'm meant to be in them or something.

"It's not your fault, you didn't make me fall off" I mumbled into his chest, I felt his softly squeeze me before he kissed the top of my head. A few weeks ago I would of probably freaked out over that little moment, but now, the Pierce brothers where just a part of my daily life, sure I still had to pinch myself to make sure this was all real. But their effect on me had worn off over the first week I had been here. I pulled away and looked up at him, his brown eyes were full of concern and worry, I gave him a soft smile, I started to turn around but before I could move, Matt's lips were on mine.

→ Chapter eleven

___

___ I sat there frozen, not knowing what to do. All my brain was doing was yelling at me to kiss him back, but I couldn't I didn't like him like this. I felt him pull away and look at me, but I sat there starring at him with a shocked expression on my face,

"I..Uh. Better go," he stuttered as he pushed himself off my bed and hurrying out the door which caused me to finally snapped out of my shock ,

"Matt! Wai.. Damn it!" I sighed as I ran my fingers throw my hair and fell back on my bed. I pulled a pillow over my head to muffle the scream I let out into it. Why did he have to do that? I sighed as I pulled the pillow off my head, I was never good with boys, I was always so awkward around them, Sarah was the person I always went to with boys...SARAH! I pulled my laptop towards me and pulled up skype. Why couldn't she be on when I needed her! I grabbed my phone off my bed side table and tapped her messages, and quickly started to type,

'Get your ass on skype now. I need to talk to you!'

'What? What's going on, everything ok?'

'Just get on skype and I'll tell you'

Within a few minutes of me sending the last text, the incoming call tone rang around my room,

"E! What's wrong?" Sarah asked, concern all over her face,

"Matt kissed me," I blurted out, ok I hadn't really wanted to start the conversation with that but I couldn't hold it in any longer,

"Oh my god! Are you serious! That is amaz... that is not good?" She wondered as I shook my head at her,

"It's not good S, I don't think I like him like that. He's my best friend here, I don't want it to be awkward!" I sighed pulling Sully into my chest, giving him a big squeeze.

"What do you mean you don't THINK you like him like that?" she asked, raising her eyebrows at me. "I don't know.. I just..It's complicated," I sighed, shaking my head,

"E, you can tell me anything," Sarah sighed, giving me a soft smile, I took a deep breath and nodded,

"The reason it's complicated is because... I don't know if I like Matt.. or Ryan."

———

I took a deep breath as I lifted my hand up and left a loud knock on Matt's bedroom door, please don't be in, please don't.. but my thoughts were interrupted when the door opened, shit.

"Hey.." I smiled, unsure of what his reaction was going to be, I wouldn't be too happy if I had just kissed someone and they had just sat there.

"Uh. Hey" he replied,

"look. I'm sorry about before, you just.. caught me off guard and I had no idea what to do!" I sighed, trying to keep myself under control, because what I'd most like to do now was hide under my blankets and never, ever come out. But Sarah convinced me that I needed to tell him the truth. He needed to know that I didn't know how I really felt about him...or his brother.

" Elena. It's fine, I get it. You don't like me like that" he sighed, shrugging his shoulders at me,

"It's not... Can we just not talk out here, can I come into your room? Please?" I asked, looking up and down the hall, hoping none was listening,

"Yeah. Ok, sure" he said before stepping aside, letting me come in. I limped into his room and stood awkwardly beside him as he closed the door behind me.

"Look. It's not that I don't like you like that. Because trust me, I actually wished I knew 100% that I liked you because you are the perfect freaking guy any girl could ask for, it's just.." I sighed, looking down at my hands, not wanting to continue the sentence that could hurt him and our friendship,

"It's just what Elena?" He asked softly, I could feel his eyes on me, I looked up at him and connected our gazes, he needed to know the truth.

"It's just.. I think.. I like someone else, as well as you." I admitted, I saw hurt cross his eyes and I'm not going to lie, it hurt me, a lot to see that I had hurt him.

"It's Ryan isn't it?" He calmly asked, the hurt no longer in his eyes. I caught my breath from his abrupt reply I hadn't been expecting that reply. I stayed silent for a while and finally slowly nodded. A tense silence fell around us both as looked we both stared at each other neither of us know what else to say,

"I think you should go Elena." Matt stated, running his hand threw his hair,

"Matt.." I asked, taking a small step towards me,

"I think you should go." He stated again, anger present in his voice, I nodded and limped over to the door, I glanced back at him and pulled open the door, I softly closed it behind me and started towards my room, I stopped short when my eyes met with the familiar ones that I didn't want to be face with at the moment.

"How much did you hear?" I asked, my voice stuttering slightly,

"I heard everything."

———

→ Chapter twelve

___ "I thought I told you to stay the fuck away from my boyfriend." She spat as she walked towards me, I took a stepped backwards, but cringed as I put weight on my ankle.

"I haven't done anything. I promise." I sighed, as Rebecca came face to face with me,

"You better not have and if you even try ANYTHING on with him. You'll wish that you'd never come here. I can make your life a living hell if I want to," she smirked as she looked me up and down,

"It's not like he'd be interested in you anyway, look at you. But just in case he has a moment of stupidity, you better stay away from him."

"That's going to be pretty hard since I LIVE with him," I retorted all I wanted was to wipe that god awful smirk off her face and it worked, the smirk slid right off of her face.

"Just stay the fuck away from him and if you do anything that I don't like, he'll find out about your stupid little crush" She spat

"Bec? What's going on?" I heard Ryan's voice ask from behind us, I felt Rebecca freeze before she plastered a sickening smile on her face before turning around to face him,

"Oh nothing, just helping Elena, she fell over. She's such a klutz." She giggled as she wrapped her arms around Ryan's waist, placing a kiss on his cheek,

"You ok Elena?" He asked, worry present in his eyes,

"I'm..fine," I mumbled, before walking past them.

"Are you sure?" I heard him ask as he wrapped his hand around my wrist stopping me in my tracks, I looked over my shoulder at him and looked down at his hand around my wrist and then back up at him, I saw Rebecca shot me a glare warning me.

"I'm fine. Just.. Leave me alone Ryan." I sighed before pulling my wrist out of his grasp and starting off towards the stairs.

———

I felt the tears that had gathered up in my eyes on the way to the barn finally begin to fall down my cheeks as I unbolted the gate to Maddie's stall, I slid in and through myself around her neck, letting the tears finally flow at a steady stream, damping her soft dappled coat. What had I gotten myself into? Why had I had to fall for both of them? I had come here to follow my dream, and I have let myself be taken over by these two guys and I hadn't even known it. I buried my face into Maddie's neck and took a deep, hitched breath as I tried to calm myself down. Everything was falling apart, things would be awkward with Matt and I can't even look at Ryan without Rebecca, telling him that I like him, and to top it all off my ankle is going to be crap for god knows how long! Everything couldn't get any worse, I don't know what I'd do if something happened to Maddie. I pulled away from Maddie and brushed the wet patched I had made on her neck softly with my hand,

"Maddie..Want am I going to do?" I sighed as I kept running my hand down her neck, she gave a contented sigh and kept on eating her hay, I couldn't help but smile slightly, she was so peaceful just eating her hay. I glanced around myself noticing everything growing darker around me, how long had I been out here?

"I better go back babe, I'll see you tomorrow ok?" I smiled as I kissed the top of her muzzle before letting myself back out the stable. I bolted the door at the top and bottom and wrapped my arms around myself as I slowly started to make my way down the aisle of the barn,

"Elena!" I heard a familiar voice yell after me, I felt my stomach churn, couldn't he just leave me alone? I kept on walking, doing my best to ignore him.

"Elena wait." He sighed as he caught up to me, wrapping his hand around my wrist he pulled me to a stop,

"I said leave me alone Ryan" I sighed as I yanked my arm around from his grasp and started walking again, knowing that he'd walk after to me but it was worth a try.

"You may as well crawl on the ground with that ankle," he laughed, trying to lighten the mood as he easily caught up to me. I sighed as I stopped and looked up at him,

"Hey..What's wrong?" He asked, worry crossing his face.

"Nothing. What do you want?" I stated, starring him straight in the eye, ignoring the butterflies that bubbled up in my stomach.

"This." He whispered before pulling me closer towards him and pressing his lips against mine.

This can't be happening again, not twice in one day. I gathered enough strength to push him off of me, as much as I hated to admit it, I didn't want to do it, I didn't want to push him off. But I couldn't go around kissing both brothers!

"You can't do that Ryan!" I shouted, pushing him in the chest again which had no effect on him what so ever, "You can't just come here and freaking kiss me!"

"Why not?" He answered softly, starring down at me, I blinked at him, was he serious?

"Last time I checked you had girlfriend." I stated, raising my eyebrows at him,

"I broke up with her. She told me everything Elena." He sighed, running his fingers through his hair. Wait.. Had he broken up with her to be with me?

"I like you Elena. I have since the day you came here," He continued as he took a step closer to me, clearing the distance I had put in-between us, "I broke up with Rebecca, because I want to be with you." I stood there frozen staring up at him, how? why? I couldn't put two words together. He cupped my face in his hands softly, I could tell he was searching for some kind of emotion in my eyes,

"Elena.." I felt him slowly close in again, this time stopping a few centimetres away, I took a deep breath and closed the few centimetres that where left, I kissed him.

_____

Please don't kill me C:

→ Chapter thirteen

Hello guys!Look I'm one day early with a chapter :D Yay, go me. Ok anyway, this chapter! My friend wrote the first part, that's all from her mind. Mwhahaha. Well I hope you enjoy this chapter! It's more horsey than anything, so will the next chapter, but there is a surprise at the end ;) Alsoo my friend has started on here and her story is amazingg so far, so go check it out! It's the external link over there ->Next Update: Sunday. - Bronxx _____

He gently pushed me against the wall, his hands were holding me by the waist. I grabbed his shirt and slide it up a little holding on to him, his lips were locked between mine. We paused with his lips still only centimetres away, I felt his breath against my lips as we looked up into each other's eyes with such passion. I smiled softly at him which he returned. He wrapped his arm around my hips and pulled me in close. Looking down at my lips, he softly touched the side of my face and kissed me again. He started to slowly sliding my shirt up as his hand slowly grasping onto my body, it was getting hotter and intense as each second went on. It felt like we were losing control, I pulled back and leaned against the wall trying to catch my breath.

He smiled softly as he softly put his forehead on mine. Tingles shot up my spine as he softly ran his hand down my arm and laced his fingers with mine. "I should go," I whispered, as I unlaced our hands and ducked under his arm he was leaning against the wall to steady himself, and before he could say anything else I was out into the cold, clear night. What had I done? I'd just hooked up with Ryan and Matt kissed me this morning. What the hell was I going to do? This just made everything even more complicated than it already was! I let out a sigh as I climbed the stairs of porch. Well, whatever I was going to do I needed to figure it out, and soon. _____

I sighed as my alarm clock blasted me with its annoying, sharp beeps. To be honest, I was already awake, I hadn't slept at all last night. I kept thinking about what I was going to do, I know Ryan would think that we'd happen. But something about him makes me not want to trust him, he seems the type of guy that would just hook up with girls and then dump them. While Matt seems more boyfriend material. But Ryan.. oh my god! Why can't it just be simple, why can't Ryan be a jerk and Matt be perfect, or Ryan be perfect and Matt be a jerk! I let out a frustrated groan as I rolled out of bed completely forgetting about my ankle, I braced for pain as I landed on my ankle. But nothing, no sharp pains, no dull aches. So much for not being able to walk on it for at least a week! I'd be able to do my first show! I smiled brightly as I grabbed cream breeches and a black polo before rushing into the bathroom, I had a lot of training to do. I'd missed out on two days already, I couldn't afford to lose anymore, and it'd help me get my mind off everything. _____

I couldn't wipe the smile off my face as I almost skipped towards Maddie's Stable. I grabbed her leather halter off the hook and slipped into her stall, "How are you today Miss Mads?" I sung as I flipped the lead rope over her neck and kissed her on her neck before slipping the halter over her nose and buckling it up. I pushed open the stable door and stepped out, Maddie following me closing behind. I pushed the door closed with my foot, making sure Maddie was out of the way and walked towards the cross-tie area. The soft clack of Maddie's shoes rung around me as we headed down the concrete aisle, that was probably one of my favourite sounds of all time. As we got to the cross-ties, I quickly clipped them onto the side of her halter and unhitched the lead rope and picked up a curry comb, getting to work on her dusty, dappled coat. By the time I had finished, her coat was gleaming and silky. I stepped back to admire how perfect she was. How had I gotten so lucky with her? Sure she probably cost half a million dollars, but she was mine, well at least for now anyway. I wiped my hand on a towel that was hanging on the wooden half wall that divided each of the 10 cross-tie bays and picked up my hunter green saddle blanket that I had laid out before I had gotten Maddie. I flicked it over her back before placing my sheepskin half pad and saddle on top. I quickly pulled up the girth, making it quite lose. I slipped on her bridle and grabbed my helmet. "Should we ride in the outdoor or the indoor today?" I whispered to Maddie as we walked down the aisle, she gave a soft snort and shook her head. I giggled slightly and nodded, "Outdoor it is!" I halted her at the wooden mounting block and tighten her girth once again, this time, securing it so it sat snugly on her. I pulled down both my stirrups and hooked my foot into the stirrup and swung over onto her back. Ahh, it felt so good to be back on top again even after only been off for two days."Elena! What do you think you're doing?!" I heard a deep voice boom at me from behind, I spun around in my saddle as saw Alan striding towards me."I'm fine, my ankle is basically back to normal!" I sighed as he reached Maddie's shoulder,"Well if it's fine, give me your 2-point position," he ordered, raising an eyebrow, I sighed and rose up. I pushed my heels down and closed into 2-point. I kept if for a while and sat upright again, I shot him a quick smile,"See, perfect!" "Ok, you proved your point. But if you start to feel even a little ache. You come right back here and get a groom to unsaddle Maddie for you. I don't want you damaging it even more," he sighed before, letting out a soft chuckle. I let out a sigh of relief in my head, I smiled at him before pressing Maddie into a walk."Hey, Elena! Wait up. I'll ride down with you!" I cringed at his voice, I had spent all this morning avoiding him after what happened last night. I just wanted to ride by myself where I could concentrate, but now it would be spoiled by Ryan's perfect, annoying face. I glanced at him and nodded, at least Matt hadn't come as well."Wait guys, I'll come with you." Shit. Spoke to soon. This was going to be one amazing ride.

→ Chapter Fourteen

H ey guys!

I'm so, so, so sorry for not updating for ages! I just started back at school this week and already have quite a bit of work :(So I'll only probably be uploading on a friday's as I have them off and Sunday :)

I promise I won't miss them, but if I do, I'll make it up to you!

Anyway, this chapter isn't the most amazing, it's more horsey than anything. The next chapter will be better, promise!

But I'll let you read on!!

Next Update: Sunday [Maybe as I'm going to look at a few horses this weeked.]

- Bron

xx

———

They couldn't just have gone and ridden in the indoor could they? They had to come down with the me to the outdoor. Sure if it was just Ryan, or just Matt it would probably be ok, I could ignore one.

But two!? Two brothers that I have both kissed, two brothers that I both like and I have no idea what I'm going to do. I was going to avoid them for as long as I could, but that only lasted a few hours. Any girl would love to be in this situation with these two perfect guys, but me? I hate drama! I let out a sigh as we reached the arena, I glanced at both of them before pressing my heels against Maddie's sides, making her erupt into her bouncy but comfortable trot. I couldn't help but smile, god I've missed this horse.

"Elena! What are you doing?!" I heard Ryan shout out after me as I trotted down to the other end of the arena,

"I'm working! You should too!" I yelled back at him over my shoulder, what a stupid question... I sighed again, I have to get my thoughts away from them, I just need to concentrate on my riding and Maddie. I quickly gathered up my plaited, leather reins as I reached the other side of the arena. I softly asked for her to soften, which she gladly took. Was there anything this horse wouldn't do? I gathered her up and did a few warm-up laps. I pushed my heels down as far as I could and sat up into my 2-point position. I should probably do no stirrup work, but to be honest, I didn't want to have dead legs tomorrow. I had made Maddie work harder than I have made her work ever before on her flat work, collections, extensions, flying changes, you name it. I did it with her. Usually I only did a quick warm up and then I'd go straight into Jumping, but I felt like I was a bit rusty with all the flat-work and it wouldn't hurt Maddie to do it. So far the boys haven't said anything to me, or even come anywhere near me. They were fooling around down on the other end of the arena, don't even ask me how they seem to win everything. Their training seems to be a few laps of trot and canter and then a few odd jumps here and there. I softly moved my weight to the back of the saddle and Maddie smoothly changed from walk to canter. I let her have a long rein as I walked down to where the guys were waiting,

"You done?" Ryan laughed, as he shifted his weight in his saddle,

"uh..no. I haven't even jumped yet." I scoffed as I kicked my feet out of my stirrups and swung myself off of Maddie, "Unlike you both, who seem to just fool around. I actually train." I continued as grabbed Maddie's reins and swung them over her head before making my way to the combination that was set up across the middle of the arena.

"Do you know how many strides are in here?" I asked, glancing back at Ryan and Matt who looked like they were about to burst out laughing, but as soon as they saw my eyes on them they quickly sobered up and looked at each other,

"I think 2 and then 1, you can change it if you want," Matt replied as squeezed his horse into a walk, making his way over to where I stood.

"Good. Because I need too."

"I'll do it, how many strides do you want?"

"umm..thanks. 2 and a half and then 1 and half. I need to work on my lengthening and shortening," I smiled as I swung my reins over her head and then quickly mounted again.

_____

I took a deep breath as I rounded the corner to the combination, I planned to go for 3 strides and then 2. I've figured that Maddie is very quick on being about to lengthen her strides but as soon as I ask for a shortened stride, it's like the whole world has ended. She gets upset and decides today isn't the day that she wants to co-operate with me. Knowing the show this weekend, they'll probably put some tricky striding in their combos. As we reached the first upright I felt her speed up slightly, but I softly half halted and made her wait, these where only about 3' 9 so if I mucked up it wouldn't be too dangerous. I felt Maddie, shift her weight to her back legs as she took the first one in her stride, like it was just a pole on the ground. I quickly, but calmly gathered her up for the second jump as she landed, land, 1, 2, 3. Perfect! I closed again as she took the rising oxer, land, 1, 2, 2 1/2.

"Shit!" I yelled as Maddie put a chip in, making an awkward jump, I quickly gathered my reins again and gave a pat on the neck, she saved my butt, I'd asked to strongly, I glanced over at Matt and Ryan who where killing themselves laughing,

"Assholes." I shout as I canter pass them again, making my way back to the combination.

"Not our fault you looked hilarious," Ryan tried to get out between his laughing, I shook my head as I turned my attention to the combination. 1, 2, 3. I closed over the first jump again and calmly gathered her up again, land, 1, 2, 3. Perfect! I gathered up my reins and softly half halted her, I felt her slow underneath me, land, 1, 2. PERFECT! I let myself close perfect over the jump and gave her a massive pat,

"Good girl!" I sing as I leave massive pats on her neck. That felt incredible! I've never gotten her to respond to me like that in combinations until now, maybe the flat work before helped her understand what I wanted from her more.

I didn't let the smile drop as pulled her to a halt as I reached the guys,

"That was better than the first time." Matt laughed as he patted his own horse,

"Are you guys actually going to do something? Or just sit here looking like spaztics?" I asked as I kicked out my stirrups.

"Well. We are going to put these puny jumps up to 5'3 and do a course. Want to do it to?" Ryan asked as he kicked his stirrups out and swung himself off of the his big, solid black warmblood.

5'3? I've only ever jumped up to 4'5, I glanced down at Maddie who wasn't even sweating, Alan did say she could jump up to 5'5 but I don't know if I was up it yet. I took a deep breath, it couldn't be that hard could it? I looked at Matt and Ryan and nodded,

"Sure..Why not?"

→ Chapter fifteen

Hello!

Wow.. It's been forever. I'm so sorry I haven't updated in ages, I just have had tons of trouble with this chapter, I've had no idea what to write. But! I got some help from Quinn [teachmehow-toequitate on tumblr] and I think everything is back up and going! So chapters will probably be up more frequently from now on :) But yeah, not 100% happy with this chapter... but I think you'll like it :) Anyway! GO READ!

- Bron

xx

———

"Any advice?" I nervously ask as I gather my reins up once again. You couldn't blame me for being nervous! This is the first time I've jumped anything this big.

"Don't die," Ryan replied, his familiar smirk crossing his face, I glared over at him, which only made him laugh,

"Thanks for that piece of wisdom Ry," I sigh as Matt pulls his horse to a halt beside me,

"Ready?" Matt asked,

"Ready as I'll ever be," I squeak as I push Maddie into a trot. I took a deep breath and softly pressed her into a canter. I took another deep breath as I rounded to the first 5'3 vertical, I'm going to die. I'm going to fall off, crack my head open and die, and it'll all be Ryan and Matts fault. I felt Maddie's weight shift her weight to her back legs and push off, I closed, trying to keep my Eq the same as it always is, I'm not going to lie, I did sort of close my eyes over the jump. But as we landed on the other side I let a huge smile cross my face, I leant forward into 2-point and tracked right to the first of two combinations.

————

"That was amazing!" I smiled as I shifted my weight backwards resulting in Maddie smoothly transitioning to a walk before I pulled her to a halt in front of Matt and Ryan.

"You looked pretty amazing to be honest, just like a pro." Matt smiled over at him, I couldn't help but smile back, sure these two guys are my weakness but I couldn't ignore them forever.

"Why don't we try a little puissance?" Ryan smirked as he looked over at Matt,

"I don't think I should. I don't want to risk mucking up and injuring Maddie for the show tomorrow, you guys can though." I replied as I patted Maddie on the neck before giving her all her rein.

"What do you think Matt? You going to wimp out?" Ryan laughed,

"Of course not. Let's go." Matt replied,

I groaned and rolled my eyes, guys, seriously. Always trying to outdo each other. I had a feeling that this wouldn't end up as well as both of them think it might.

———

So far so good, 6'2 and still going strong,

"How about we just put it up to 7ft now?" Ryan smiled as he swung himself off of his horse and made his way to the jump, putting it up a few holes.

"You're on your own Ryan, I don't even want to attempt that." Matt sighed as he let his horse have a long rein,

"Fine suit yourself, I'll just do it on my own," Ryan smirked as he quickly mounted again,

"Ry, I don't think you should do it, you could mess it up, badly." I sighed, looking over at him,

"I'll be fine. But thanks for worrying about me El," He laughed, giving me a wink before pressing his horse into a canter. I groaned, I can't watch this, I covered my eyes and peeked between the gaps between my fingers. He turned the corner to the set up oxer, clearing it by miles, I saw his horse back off slightly before the jump but he pushed it forwards. That should of been his first clue to give up, if the horse wasn't willing to do it, then it's most likely that it probably won't be willing to jump it. I gasped and covered my eyes fully as I saw Ryan and his horse, skidding to a stop in front of the jump. I heard poled falling down, crashing on top of each other, I glanced between the gaps again and saw Ryan's horse struggling on his knees, before pulling himself up so he was standing, he stood there shaking, luckily

Ryan had stayed on but he quickly jumped off, going to the front of his horse.

"Shit!" I heard his sigh,

"What the hell happened?!" I heard Alan's voice boom over at us, I glanced behind me and saw Alan striding towards his son.

"Nothing. I just got the striding wrong," Ryan sighed as his father reached him,

"Ryan. Your horses knees are grazed almost down to the bone" He yelled, as he examined Ryan's horses knees,

"How the hell did that even happen?" He questioned as he turned to his son once again,

"We were doing puissance and Ryan decided he'd be able to jump 7ft." Matt piped up, seeming as Ryan had gone silent,

"You both a stupid and reckless! Two things that don't go well together with having horses! Ryan. You are not going to that show tomorrow, firstly because your horse is going to be out of action for god knows how long! AND just because I said so, so go up to the barn and clean him up. I'll call the vet." Alan huffed as he stalked up towards the barn office,

"You're such an idiot Ryan." Matt sighed as he pushed his horse into a walk and calmly walked up to the barn, I sighed and jumped off of Maddie and flipped the reins over her head, I slowly made my way towards Ryan who was cursing under his breath,

"Come on, you have to clean his legs up. No use standing here swearing at yourself." I smiled softly as I put my hand on his arm. He glanced at me and then at my hand, and nodded.

"Looks like I'll just be your groom tomorrow then," He smirked as we started to walk slowly up to the barn.

Oh yay.

→ Chapter sixteen

Hii there :)New Chapter and it isn't like ages apart from the previous chapter :)I don't know what to say about this chapter other than I had fun writing it and it's a lot! longer than usual :P I had to make it up to you some how!Next Update: Friday or earlier.-Bronxx_____

"Wakey, wakey! IT'S THE BIG DAY!" I heard someone shout in my ear,

"WHAT THE HELL RYAN!" I screamed as I fell out of bed landing on my back, starring up at the smirking face of Ryan,"Good morning to you to Elena," He smiled as he held out his hand towards me, I glared at him but reluctantly took his hand. He pulled me up, pulling me into his chest before wrapping his arms around my waist,"Uh-hum. Please remove your arms from around my waist before I knee you where no boy likes to be kneed," I threatened which made him quickly retracted his arms from around my waist,"So moody, is it your time of the month?" He smirked,"Get out!" I shouted as I pushed him towards the door before giving him one last shove before slamming the door shut in his face. He's such a jerk. I let out

a groan and ran my fingers through my hair before glancing at my
bedside clock, 3am. This was going to be one long day. _____

I let out a sigh as I bit into my apple as I made my way towards the
already bustling barn, I stepped inside and felt a rush of excitement
run through me, this was my first show with Maddie, and I was
going to make sure it was one to remember! I smiled at a few people
as I walked down the aisle of the stables. I swear almost everyone
here was going, and that's about 100 people maybe even more. "You
ready Mads?" smiled as I reached her stall, I held out the core of the
eaten apple I had in my hand which she happily ate, I grabbed her
halter off of the hook and slipped into her stall,"Ohh, look at your
pretty plaits! They stayed in really well," I smiled to myself as I slipped
on her supple brown leather halter,"We're going to kick butt today.
Everyone won't know what has hit them," I whispered to her as we
made our way out of the stall and over to the cross-tie area. I grabbed
my brushes and set to work, making sure there was no sign or dust
or dirt or any unwanted things left on her dappled body. I smiled as I
stepped back to examine her, perfect, as always."You could of gotten
me to do that you know," I heard Ryan chuckle as he reached my side,
I felt my heart rate quicken as our hands brushed each other, why the
hell did he effect me that much from just a brush? I glanced up at him
and let a smile cross my face but I quickly second guessed myself and
looked back at Maddie, who was half-asleep."No, I like grooming, it
relaxes me," I replied before walking over to the four hunter green
and navy shipping boots sat along with a matching cooler, I picked
up the shipping boots and quickly wrapped them around her legs,

securing them snugly. I glanced over at Ryan again who was staring at me, he smiled when he saw my eyes on him, a genuine smile, it made him look even more irresistible. Shit! Elena no. Stop. You have to concentrate on the show, not Ryan, not Matt. Matt.. I still have to talk to him. I let out a sigh as I tore my eyes away from him, I quickly threw on the Blanket and buckled it up."Elena.." I jumped as I heard Ryan whisper in my ear, how did he even get over here that quickly?"Y-yeah?" I stuttered as I realized how close he was, once again,"I take it you're not a morning person," he whispered, I glanced up at him and saw that his usual smirk was plastered over his face, god he was a jerk,"You're a jerk," I whispered back at him my eyes narrowing, of course I'll be a bitch when you scream in my ear,"But you love it," he whispered once again his breath hot on my skin, which sent tingles down my spine. I looked up at him, his eyes starred into mine, I let my eyes wonder down to his lips, Elena.. What are you doing? I thought to myself, but I couldn't push him away. I felt his arm snake around my waist as he pulled me closer into him, I caught my breath as I felt his body against mine , I willed myself to push away but it wasn't working, my brain had shut off. He looked down at me before he pressed his lips against mine. What the hell am I doing? I haven't even talked to Matt yet! This was his brother, his twin that I was kissing, for the second time! This shouldn't be happened. But then why wasn't I stopping it, I could easily push him away. And why did it feel so right when I was with him, yes he made me so angry most of the time but.. I just can't explain it."Elena! Where are you? It's time to get going," I heard one of the grooms shout towards us from down the aisle of the stable, my brain quickly started working again and I gathered enough strength to push Ryan and myself apart. I heard him let out a sigh as I turned around and quickly snapped off both of the clips that where clipped onto Maddie's halter, I grabbed her rope and attached it,"I'm coming!" I yelled back before looking at Ryan over my shoulder, I let out a sigh before pulling softly on Maddie's lead rope before walking down the aisle towards the floats and trucks that waited outside. _____

2 hours. That's how long it took us to get to the show, and for those two hours I was stuck in the car with Ryan, it was the most awkward drive I've ever been on. "Elena we need to talk," Ryan finally said as we pulled into the showground, I stayed silent for a while, before finally speaking up,"You're right.. But," "But what?" "But..I have to concentrate on the show. I don't need you messing with my head even more, and I need to think about you.." I sighed before I pushed open the door, not waiting for Ryan to answer. I stood outside the car for awhile, surveying what was going on, many people where already warming up for the first class that would start in 10 minutes. In front of me were 3 picture perfect barns for the horses that where competing to stay in between classes and overnight, to my left where 4 competition rings, all full of stunning courses, and finally to my right there were two massive Olympic sized arenas dedicated to warming up, I couldn't help but let my mouth drop, this was amazing, I couldn't believe I was here. At one of the first top events in America, one where almost all of the top riders ride. Luckily my class wasn't until 10 and I was the 20th person to go so I probably

wouldn't be on until 10:20 and it was only 7 now so I had plenty of time to check in and grab my number, get changed and get Maddie tacked up and warmed up. I looked over at Ryan once more but he was already surrounded by girls, all mobbing for his attention, another reason why I had to think about him, I don't know how I'd handle seeing girls basically throwing themselves at him at every horse show we go too. I sighed and shoved my hands in my jumper pockets before making my way towards the truck where they had already unloaded Maddie. _____

Damn him and his stupid being. I wasn't able to get Ryan out of my head all morning, and did I mention I had never seen him today without a pack of horse show girls stalking him and to make it worse! Yes. It can get worse, I had seen him flirting with quite a few of them, who does he think he is?! Does he think he can just kiss me, say we should talk and then go off a flirt with some other girls, god I hate him! I hate what he's doing to me, I never get jealous, ever!"Need any help?" I heard his voice sound out from behind me, I placed my saddle on top of the white saddle blanket and cream fluffy and smoothly tightened the girth,"Not from you," I snipped back, before grabbing my bridle off the hook, probably a bit harder than I should of, and flipping the reins over Maddie's head,"What is wrong with you?" He said, I could tell that he was smirking,"Nothing is wrong with me Ryan. You're the one with the problem," I scoffed as I pulled the bridle over Maddie's ears, making sure not to mess up her forelock plait,"I have a problem?" "Just piss off!" I whispered angrily as I slipped Maddie's halter over her halter, I sat down on my tack truck and pulled on my Parlanti boots,"Not until you talk to me," He sighed as he gave Maddie a pat on the neck before bending underneath it and making his way to sit next to me on my tack truck,"Go talk to the mob of girls waiting outside for you," I scoffed as I grabbed my number and started to try and tie is around my waist, but my fingers didn't seem to be able to function,"Let me," Ryan said as he took the material between his fingers and quickly secured it around my small waist, "You know, you sound a little bit jealous," "Well I'm not," I lied"You're an awful liar you know," "I'm not lying!" "You know you're kind of hot when you're mad," he chuckled, I turned around and stared at him,"You want to help me?" I sighed as I unbuckled Maddie's halter before slipping it off of her head, "Can you take Maddie outside, let her munch some grass while I put on my hair-net" I sighed before taking the reins up and over her head before holding them out to Ryan, he looked at me softly and nodded before taking them from him, once again causing our skin to brush against one another's, I quickly pulled my hand away and turned away from him. I let out a breath as I heard Maddie's hoof beats turn from a sharp click to the soft thud on grass, I needed to stop letting him get to me, I needed to focus on Maddie and only Maddie. I grabbed my hair-net and looked in front of the mirror that was on top of my trunk, I tucked in a few short hairs that I had missed and pulled on my GPA first lady.

––––––

"1,2,3 up." Ryan counted before he helped me up onto Maddie's back, I had about half an hour before it was my turn in the ring and Maddie needed almost all that time to get warmed up, I found she jumped better when I had put a solid half hour warm-up into her. "Thanks," I mumbled to Ryan as I softly pressed my spurs into Maddie's side, pushing her into a walk. "My dad would help you warm up but.. he's busy with Matt at the moment, so you're stuck with me," Ryan finally said as we reached the first warm up arena that was bustling with riders warming up for the 3 other classes that were going on at the same time as mine. I nodded at him and pressed Maddie into her springy trot, leaving Ryan on the sideline of the arena. Collections, extensions, flexing, transitions, leg-yielding, I put Maddie through her paces making sure she was supple and listening 100% to me before I even attempted one of 5 warm-up jumps set up in the middle of the arena, I glanced over at Ryan who was now in the middle of the arena talking with a few other people, I trotted over to him and as I pulled up beside him he turned to face me, "Could you put that vertical in the middle down about a hole, and then raise it again after I jump it," I asked, he nodded in return and made his way over to the jump, checking first with a few people and then put it down. I gathered Maddie up and asked for a halt to canter transition, which she did perfectly. I turned the corner and waiting for the jump to come to me, I didn't push her and I didn't hold her, I let Maddie sort out the striding. I felt her shifter her weight backwards and push off the ground, I closed, keeping my eyes up, heels down, lower leg on the girth. I gave her a quick pat before I gathered her up again to jump it again, now that Ryan had put it up. So far so good, every practise fence we had done, we did perfectly and I had maintained my perfect eq, now it all depended on my actual round. "Rider 145! You're in next!" I heard someone called from across the rider. It was my turn next, I suddenly felt the butterflies erupt in my stomach, why couldn't they had not come at all, I didn't feel like dealing with nerves as well at the Ryan issue. I let Maddie have a long rein as Ryan and I made out way silently to my class. I watched silently as the rider before me completed her round, from what I watched I could tell she was an amazing rider, not to mention her horse, her horse was amazing! It cleared the 3'9 fences by almost a foot. The crowd erupted as she crossed the finish, why couldn't I have gone after someone who had sucked, now my nerves had gotten even worse. "Good riding Mimi." Ryan smiled at the girl who had just ridden out of the arena, he knew her? Of course he knew her look at her! She was perfect. "Thank you so much Ryan! Why aren't you riding?" She smiled before jumping off her horse, and handing it to who I think was one of her grooms, "Well, my horse went down yesterday so I'm out," he sighed, "Now we have rider 145, Elena Moore, riding Take flight who is owned by The Pierce family," I heard the speaker boom out around the arena I took a deep breath and started to gather my reins before I felt a hand on my thigh, I looked down at Ryan who smiled up at me, "You'll do great," He smiled, why did he have to do that, I had finally gotten my thoughts under control, I had no Ryan in my head, but now, Ryan was all that I could think of. I smiled back at him and pressed Maddie into a trot as I entered the ring.

→ Chapter seventeen

A NOTHER CHAPTER?! I am on a roll C:

Apperticate it as much as you can, It probably won't happen again ahahha.

Video over there -> is what I based Elena's round off, I just added a few things to make it fit my storyline ;) It's just the first round so it stops around 1:30.

Not the best chapter I don't think.. But oh well!

READ ON!

- Bron

xx

———

I took a shaky breath as I rounded the corner to the first of 11 jumps, with two doubles.

It was only a rising oxer, one of the jumps Maddie finds the most easiest so she took it in her stride, like it was only a small vertical, I gathered her up as we approached one of the many verticals, it should be a perfect 7 strides, land, 1, 2, 3, 4, 5, 6, 7, perfect! I sat back quickly and gathered her up again, as I rolled back to another simple vertical, I felt Maddie pull against me but I softly pulled back,

"Stop it, not yet." I whispered down to her as we cantered a long, sweeping turn to the first of two doubles, this double faced the exit, the place where the horse wants to go the most, I felt Maddie pick up speed again my I quickly shut it down, I looked forward and took a deep breath, my eyes wandered a bit, they fell on Ryan, who was still talking to that Mimi girl, I cursed myself as I felt made take off for the first jump and I closed with her, it wasn't a long spot or a short one, Maddie had taken me to it, I took a deep breath and quickly gathered her up, land, 1 ,2, 2 1/2, shit. I felt Maddie chip, saving my butt. Luckily she gave an extra kick over the jump, saving us a fault, I sighed as I gave her a pat. Elena, you really have to focus. I maintained a steady even rhythm as we approached another rising oxer, which Maddie soared over. I felt her quicken once again as she saw the next jump in sight, I gave a sharp yank on her mouth, a bit harder than I meant to which made her suddenly slow down, I had to quick a quick squeeze as I pushed to get over the jump. I braced for the thud of a rail hitting the arena but it never came, I took a deep breath as I set her up with another roll back to another vertical, she popped it nicely. We took another long, sweeping corner to one of the trickiest jumps on the course, a triple bar that had 6 1/2 stride coming to it out of the corner, I planned to do 6 when I had walked the course earlier with Alan, so I kept my leg on and rode strongly, but Maddie took it the wrong way and took a long spot, unbalancing me and made me lose both of my stirrups. I panicked slightly as I tried to get my feet back into my stirrups but it only confused Maddie, she sped up but I slowed her down and forgot about my hanging stirrups,

"Sorry girl," I sighed as I did my best to gather her up again before the next jump, but it came quickly and caused Maddie to take another long spot, unbalancing me once again,

"Fuck!" I whispered angrily as we landed on the other side, I groaned at myself and gathered her up again and turned her a bit too quickly, I felt her faultier underneath me, like her legs were about to give way, but she corrected my mistake, once again and continued like nothing happened. I cursed under my breath again as I gathered her up and held her, waiting for the next double to come to us, land, 1, 2, perfect. I gathered her for the last jump and pushed her on, making her clear the 5 strides out of the corner to the final jump in no time. I gave her a big pat as we crossed the finished, that wasn't how I wanted my first show to go.

I sighed as I let myself fall back onto my tack trunk after untacking and washing Maddie for the third and finally time. What an awful day, my first class was a disaster and it only got worse from there, in my second class I knocked down 2 rails and got a few time penalties and in my final class I had been disqualified. I know it was all my fault, Maddie had only done what I had told her to do, but if it wasn't for Ryan, none of this would of happened! If he had only kept his hands to himself I would of been able to concentrate.

"What has been up with you today Elena?" I heard Alan sigh as he stepped out of the stable next to me, leading one of the horses he was riding today. I shrugged,

"I don't know. I just wasn't thinking straight I guess."

"Yeah. I could see that. You made fool out of yourself, you're a better rider than that."

"I know..I just...It wasn't my day," I sighed again as I leant my head back on the wooden door of Maddie's stall.

"Come on, we're heading back now. Get Maddie out and get her ready, I'll meet you out front in 10." He smiled softly before walking out the arch of the barn.

I let out a groan as I picked up all of Maddie's things and placed them in my Tack Trunk, I grabbed her shipping boots and blankets and quickly put them on her before grabbing the lead and clipping it on her halter,

"I'm sorry girl. It's all my fault our first show was a bust," I said as I lead her out of the barn and to the truck that was waiting.

Instead of driving back with Ryan, I decided to go with Alan in the truck, to save myself from having to face Ryan. I don't know what I'd do to him if I had saw him after my last round.

———

I let out a frustrated groan as I threw the scoopful of lucence into the bucket of feed,

"What did the feed ever do to you?" I heard someone laugh from the doorway,

"Go away Ryan. I'm not in the mood." I snapped throwing a handful of sunflower seeds in,

"Good thing I'm not Ryan then,"

I looked up and saw Matt leaning against the door-frame, trying his hardest not to laugh,

"Oh. Sorry I didn't know it was you," I sighed as I picked up the feed bucket, throwing it under the tap and wetting it slightly,

"Obviously. You ok?" He asked as he wondered over to me, as I mixed the feed around in the bucket,

"Yeah..Just annoyed I guess," I frowned as I looked up at him, he was a lot different than Ryan, a good different, he was a jerk for one thing. But he had kinder eyes and softer features,

"Ryan told me what happened," I tensed at his name and shook my head,

"Did he now?"

"Yeah he did.. I'm sorry El, I knew you wanted your first show to be one to remember, and not the reasons you remember it for now."

"Matt. Stop." I sighed, looking down at the ground,

"What?"

"Stop being nice to me. I...I Don't deserve it ok."

"What are you talking about?" He questioned,

I took a deep breath. It's now or never.

"Ryan kissed me, and... I kissed him back... and I think I like him"

"right..."

"Matt..I'm sorry I didn't mean.."

"Just don't Elena ok. You knew I liked you, and you go after my brother.. Just like everyone else." He sighed "Just forget it."

"Matt.."

"No Elena." He stated before turning around and walking out the door of the feed room.

God. This day just keeps getting better and better.

→ Chapter eighteen

Hello!!

This is more of a filler chapter to be honest, but it's cute C: uhmm I don't know what to say really ahaha, if you have any suggestions about this story don't be afraid to message me on here or my tumblr! [the external link over there -> if you didn't come from tumblr :)] I'd love to see where you think this story could go! Also feedback would be amazing! :D

Now I shall let you go read!

- Bron

xx

─────

This day would have to be the worst day I have ever had. First the awful show and then Matt... I'm an awful person. I uncrossed my arms across my chest as I stepped onto the soft carpet of my bedroom. I had been up for a total of 18 hours, and I couldn't wait to get to sleep. I grabbed my pj's and walked into the bathroom, I switched on the lights and closed the door behind before getting rid of the sweaty, dirty show clothes. I stepped into the shower and switched on the water, letting the scalding water wash over me.

———

I felt myself start to finally drift off to sleep as I heard a soft knock on the door, I groaned as I let my eyes flutter open. I hate everyone. I slipped out of my warm comfy bed, and padded towards the door, I opened it and stared at Ryan,

"What do you want?" I sighed as I leaned against the door frame,

"I wanted to say that I'm sorry," he said softly, I looked at him and raised my eyebrows,

"What are you sorry for?"

"I'm sorry for being such a jerk. I know it was my fault you screwed up today. If I hadn't had kissed you this morning. You would of rode like you always do." He explained, I couldn't help but let a smile creep up, as much as I had hated him for what happened at the show today, and what happened between Matt and I. I knew it took a lot of him to come and say sorry,

"Why are you smiling? I expected you to yell at me or cry or some thing.." He asked confusedly

"I talked to Matt.."

"oh."

"Yeah.."

"What did you say?"

"I said.. That I liked you,"

"What?"

"I said that I like you,"

I saw his eyes light up, and another genuine smile cross his face, this boy was going to be the end of me, he took a step towards me, his smile still tugging at the corners of his lips,

"So. Does that mean I can kiss you without feeling like I'm doing something wrong?" He smiled, softly cupping both hands around my neck, bringing his own face closer to mine. I nodded and smiled,

"It most defiantly means..." But before I could finish Ryan crashed his lips on top of mine, and I finally let myself got lost it in.

———

I don't think my smile has ever left my face from what happened last night, everything was so wrong and confusing when the day began and it got worse as the day went on, but by the end, everything felt right again. I was with Ryan and I could finally concentrate on my riding without any distractions. I smiled even bigger as I walked into the tack room of the barn to see a familiar back turned towards, hunched over a saddle, I snuck up behind him and wrapped my arms around his neck, planting a kiss on his cheek,

"Morning!" I chirped as Ryan quickly glanced sideways, a smile spread across his face when he saw it was me,

"Hey," He smiled as he turned around on his stool, pulling me by my breeches belt loops towards him, positioning me so I was standing between his legs, I smiled as I leant down and pecked his lips,

"What ya doing?" I sung as I looked behind him at the 5 saddles that sat behind him,

"My dad put me on saddle cleaning duty because of the stunt I pulled," he laughed,

"Well that's good, you could of killed Fons OR yourself," I frowned as I softly slapped him

"owww," he groaned as rubbed his face, pretending that is actually hurt. I giggled slightly and stepped backwards,

"Come on. Get cleaning, I'll see you later," I winked, before moving away from him,

"Oh no you don't!" He laughed as he stood up from his chair and wrapped his arms my waist before pulling me back into the tack room,

"Ryan! I have to find out what your dad wants me to do today!" I laughed as I tried to struggle away from him, but it only made him tighten his grip on me,

"Not until I get a real good morning," he whispered into my ear, sending tingles down my spine. I stopped struggling and turned around in his arms and wrapped my arms around his neck,

"You want a real good morning? Didn't I do that?" I smiled as I looked up at him,

"No you didn't." He stated, leaning his face closer to mine. I rolled my eyes and pulled him into a kiss.

"Woah. I don't need that first thing in the morning, thank you very much." Amelia, Ryan's younger sister stated as she walked into the tack room, giving us a disgusted look.

"Sorry," I laughed as I pushed against Ryan's chest, backing away from him,

"I'll see you later ok?"

"Uh, fine, Dad wants me to exercise Rue so I'll see you," He replied, giving me one last kiss before I turned away,

"Elena and Ryan, sitting in a tree.." I heard Amelia begin to sing as I walked away from the tack room,

"Piss off will you," I heard Ryan reply, I shook my head and laughed as I continued my way towards the stable office.

→ Chapter nineteen

H ELLO!

    NEW CHAPTER YAYY. Another cute one C:

I think I have to hurry this story along a bit! The next chapter is number 20 :O Holy moly. Anyway, yeah I think in the next chapter I'll hurry it along, you'll see how :D

So here you go! I hope you enojy this one!

GO READD!

- Bron

xx

———

I let out a sigh as I put the last of the seven horses Alan had gotten me to ride today back in his stall. As much as I love riding and spending time with horses, functioning on 3 hours sleep isn't the best idea for me. Only about half an hour before I can go sleep, but at least I can chill with Maddie for a little while. I quickly hung the halter on the hook beside the stable door and started to make my way towards the riders barn where Maddie was kept.

As I walked into the barn I breathed in the familiar mix of horse, hay, sweat, leather cleaner and fresh sawdust, some people would of been put off by the smell, but not me. It would have to be one of the calming smells in the world to me. I walked slowly down the barn aisle looking in a few stalls and rooms, Ryan had said he'd be around here all day. I'd seen him a few times throughout the day doing chore after chore, but when I actually want to see him. He's nowhere to be seen,

"Hey baby," I smiled as I reached Maddie's stall. She let out a soft nicker as she made her way to the gate, I pressed my lips onto her soft muzzle and pulled out a peppermint,

"How are you today after our not so perfect first show?" I grinned as she softly took the peppermint from my stretched out palm,

"Of course. You could probably careless about winning or completely failing hey?" I laughed as Maddie retreated back to her hay bin that hung next to her feed bin.

"Hey" a husky voice whispered in my ear as I felt arms circle around my waist, I let a smile creep up as I placed my arms over his,

"Hey, I was just looking for you," I smiled as I leant back against him,

"That's good, because I was looking for you. Want to go for a trail ride?" He asked as he rested his chin on top of my head, yes. That is how short I am.

"Has your dad freed you from all the chores now has he?" I laughed as I watched Maddie contently munch on her hay,

"I only have to ride Rue, and a trail ride will be just fine since she had a show yesterday," He explained,

"I'll get Maddie ready and meet you outside in 10?" I asked as I pulled away from his arms before turning around to face him,

"Sounds like a plan, see you in 10." He said as he kissed the top of my head. He started walking away but turn around to face me once again,

"Oh. Also. Bareback," he said before giving me a smirk as he retreated down to the other end of the barn. Bareback? I smiled to myself as I grabbed Maddie's halter off the hook before slipping in with her. Why would he insist I go bareback? Guess I'll find out.

––––––

"So why exactly did you insist Maddie goes bareback?" I asked as I walked up to where he was holding his horse with his usual smirk on his face,

"Oh you'll see Elena," He chuckled as he walked over to me, I turned around and bent my leg up, signalling him to give me a leg up. He rolled his eyes and threw me up onto Maddie like I weighed nothing,

"One thing you should know. I hate surprises," I grumbled as he hoisted himself up onto Rue who was a pretty liver chestnut who looked around 16.2 hands.

"Oh I don't think you'll hate this one," he smiled as he pressed Rue into a walk, which I mirrored quickly.

We rode in comfortable silence for a while, only being able to hear the soft thud of the horses hooves and the occasional snort from both horses. The Pierce's property was amazing, I'd never seen the whole property before, there were a total of 3 barns, one for The Pierce's riders and 2 for boarders, 3 outdoor arenas and 2 indoors, and the paddocks were all pristine, wooden rails, automatic water troughs and a stable/shelter in each one. Basically it is every equestrians dreams.

"Ok, close your eyes." Ryan said, breaking the silence, I looked at him and raised my eyebrows,

"Are you crazy?! I have awful balance with my eyes closed! I'll fall off!" I panicked, but I saw Ryan's lips curve into a smile,

"Does my panicking make you happy?" I asked as he backed his horse next to me,

"Slightly," He smirked, drawing closer to me,

"Jerk," I mumbled, narrowing my eyes at him,

"Trust me?" He whispered as he softly kissed me,

"Uh. Fine, but if I fall off and di.." I threatened but was cut off by another kiss,

"You won't die. I'll lead Maddie, but it's only a few steps behind there," He laughed as he pointed at the barn beside us,

"Fine, just go slow ok."

"Ok promise, hold on," he laughed as took Maddie's reins in his hands before softly pulling her to a walk along with his horse. I sighed as I closed my eyes, only being able to rely on my other senses.

―――――

It felt like forever before I felt Maddie slow to a halt,

"Can I open my eyes yet?" I asked, jutting out my bottom lip, I heard Ryan let out a laugh,

"Yes. You can," he laughed. I finally opened my eyes, revealing a glistening lake,

"Of course! You have a lake on your property!" I laughed as I looked over at him and gave him a smile,

"Well, since I thought it was a hot day..." He started but I looked over at him and smiled,

"On your marks, get set, go!" I shouted before pushing Maddie into a canter, and into the water, not caring about my jodhpurs or shirt.

→ Chapter twenty

Not much to say other than you might hate me at the end xD-Bronxx

It has been a month and a half since Ryan had taken me down to the lake, and since then it has become a little tradition of ours. The day after we get back from a show, we'd ride bareback down to the lake and spend almost all day out there together, just letting ourselves relax and have fun. It has also been a month and a half since we got together, and we've never been stronger. It's one of those relationships you dream of, but never actually expect to happen, over the past month I've fallen for him. I'm completely and utterly in love with Ryan Pierce, who thought that, that would of happened? And I'm also taking the equestrian world by storm, Who would of thought that would happen? A few months ago, I was just another girl, dreaming about what it would be like to be riding at top level, and now, here I was being one of the most known person in the equestrian world, why? Because, apart from my first show, I've won almost every class I have entered."Elena?" A deep voice spoke from my door, snapping out of my thinking. I glanced up and felt guilt

wash over me, I forced a smile,"Hey.." I sighed, "Matt, I'm reall.."
"Elena stop. It's fine," He said as he walked over to my bed before
sitting down on the corner so he was facing me, I swung around on
my chair and my eyes locked on his soft brown ones, "It's not fine, I
hurt you! I'm going out with your twin brother, how can it be fine?"
I questioned, "Because I know that you care about him, a lot. I can
see it when you two are together. I just want you to be happy, and if
Ryan makes you happy then great, sure I'll wonder what it would be
like if we were going out but that's just in a wonder," He smiled, I felt
a smile creep up on my face and I got up and sat beside him,"You're a
cliché Matt. You know that?" I laughed softly as I looked over at him,
he shook his head and let out a small chuckle, "Friends?" I asked, "Of
course Lee," he laughed as he wrapped his arms around me, enclosing
me into a tight, warm hug. Sure they weren't Ryan's hugs, but it
made the guilt drain away. I let out a contented sigh as I pulled away,
I had my best friend back, it would take a while to get back to where
we were but I had him back, everything was even more perfect. "Oh,
by the way. Dad wanted to let you know, he's entered you in the
ENCANA Cup FEI at the Masters next Friday." I froze, was he
serious? That will be one of the biggest classes I have ever been in.
I stared at him with my mouth hanging open. I tried to speak but I
couldn't get any words out. "Bu..But." I stuttered before I cleared my
throat,"I can't do that! I'll completely fail like my first show! I've never
jumped that high before at a show" I panicked as through myself
back on my bed and covered my face with my hands,"Well you better
get practising then shouldn't you? Come on Dad is waiting for you

down in the main indoor, since it's decided to bucket down with rain" He laughed as the weight on the bed shifted, signalling he had gotten up, I let out a groan as I felt Matt pulling me up off of the bed.

———

"Come round and pop over this vertical. Make sure she's between your hand and leg, don't even think about coming to it if you feel she gets strong, circle and then come towards it again." Alan yelled at me from the viewing platform above the main indoor arena, so far this had been a disaster. I don't know if it was me being distracted by the amount of people that had decided to watch me ride, or the fact that Maddie was playing up because of the constant loud pang when each rain drop hit the roof of the indoor. But either way, I wasn't riding my best we kept chipping in, we rushed to the fences, you name everything that could go wrong, it did. I let out a sigh as I held Maddie between my hands and legs. I took a deep breath as I circled around to the 1.60m vertical that was in the middle of the arena, I waited, hold, hold, hold, release. I felt Maddie take off on the perfect spot and we clear the jump with about a few inches to spare, I let a large smile cross my face as I pulled her up to a walk,"Leave it on a good note! Cool her down and the put her away. Good job Elena," Alan yelled at me again before disappearing into the lounge that off to the right of the viewing spot. After I had walked Maddie around on a loose rein for about twenty minutes I swung my legs over her and landed on the ground, I gave her a soft rub on the neck before flipping the reins over her head and ambled back to the barn."I heard you did amazing today," Ryan smirked as he leant against the stable door where I had just put Maddie back into I scoffed and shook my head, "Who told you that lie?" "Just everyone that was watching, which was quite a few of the boarders," He laughed as wiggled his eyebrows,"You are a freaking weirdo you know that?" I laughed as I pushed against the door of the stable, but Ryan smirked and pushed back,"Ryan! Let me out," I laughed as I pushed against the door more,"Ok. Whatever you say," He smirked again as he moved away from the door as I gave it another push, I stubbled slightly and glared at him,"Jerk," I grumbled as I closed the stable door behind me, "But, I'm your jerk," He laughed as he wrapped his arms around me, before leaving a soft kiss on my lips,"You make it so hard to be mad at you, you know?" I laughed as I looked up at him, a small smile on his face. I couldn't believe that he was mine, and I was his. "Elena!" I heard a loud voice call my name, I let out a laugh as I pulled away from Ryan who frowned and rolled his eyes,"Yeah?!" I called back,"Someone is here to see you! They are out front!" I looked over at Ryan and raised my eyebrows but he shrugged at me,"How am I meant to know who it is?" He laughed as we walked down towards the front entrance of the barn. Excitement fluttered up inside of me as I saw a familiar male figure standing talking to Alan, as I got closer I saw the messy, bed head, sandy blonde hair boy that I had grown up with all my life, I let out a squeal as I ran towards him and wrapped my arms around his neck, pulling him into a bone crushing hug,"ZAC! What are you doing here?!"

→ Chapter twenty-One

Hey guys!

I'm so, so, so sorry that this is so late! Holy moly I just haven't had time to write that much and what I did write I hated so I keep starting over, ugh it was crazy! But yeah chapter 21 is here, FINALLY! I wanted to thank you for all the messages I get about TPB on tumblr, I swear if you guys didn't message me about this chapter I would of probably forgotten to write this chapter at all! SO KEEP THEM COMING, I don't find them annoying at all, so don't think that :) okie so I tried something a little bit different for this chapter, I wrote it in Ryan's point of view. I actually have no idea if this worked or not to be honest, so message me and tell me what you think about it, HONESTY! If I get a few messages saying it failed, then I might re-write it in Elena's point of view :) External link over there is where you can message me-> if you didn't come from tumblr :) Or you have leave me a comment below or message me on here :) ANYWAY I shall let you go read this long awaited chapter in peace!

I'm also sorry it's quite short! But it gives you enough to spaz and cry about ;)

NOW GO READ!

- Bron

xx

P.S Picture over there is Zac ;)

——

Ryan's POV

"ZAC?! WHAT ARE YOU DOING HERE?" I heard Elena squeal as she ran towards the dirty blonde headed guy that stood in the barn doorway. I clenched my jaw and felt my hands tighten into fists, what the hell was wrong with me? Ryan Pierce doesn't get jealous, people get jealous of Ryan Pierce. What was this girl doing to me? I don't even know this guy, for all I know he could be her brother. I cleared my throat and walked to Elena's side. I wrapped my arm around her waist and pulled her closer and gave the guy a once over,

"Ryan, this is Zac, Zac this is.." Elena started a smile still over her face,

"Ryan, her boyfriend," I smirked, looking down at her and planting a kiss on the top of her head, I heard Elena give a little giggle as she squirmed out of my arms, I put my hand out towards him which he took in a strong hand shake.

"Ok guys. Stop it, you look like you're going to kill each other any second. Ryan this is Zac, he's my best friends brother, he's the brother I never had." She explained as she smiled between me and Zac,

"But you have a brother?" He said in a thick British accent, of course. He's fucking British,

"Exactly. He's a Jerk. But we aren't going to go into that. You still haven't answered my question! What are you doing here?!" She laughed, hitting him playfully on the arm, I stood there and raised my eye brow at both of them, I swear I could of been invisible. I wouldn't been surprised if they had history together, well I would actually bet something has happened between them,

"I'm actually picking up a horse and Sarah told me you where working here, you didn't tell me El." He laughed, slinging an arm around her shoulders. I tightened my hands into fists again, god I really need to stop being jealous. I watched them babble together before I caught my dad in the corner of my eye stalking towards us,

"Elena, What are you doing, standing here talking to Zac! Hey Zac," He sighed, shaking hands with Zac, "I need you to go feed a few horses, they are written up on the board in the tack room. Ryan can help you too." He continued before gesturing down the aisle of the stable towards the tack room. Elena let out a groan and grabbed my hand before dragging me towards the tack room. I stayed silent as she bustled around the tack room, chattering about things that I couldn't hear. All I could think about was that damn Zac,

"Ryan?" I heard her ask as she wrapped her arms around my neck, pulling me to face her, I looked down at her brown, chocolate eyes and took a deep breath,

"Did anything happen between you and that Zac guy?" I asked her straight out looking down at her, a few emotions crossed her face but her face broke out in a smile,

"Oh god no. He's like my brother, that would've been so...awkward! Like dating my brother. You have nothing to worry about Ry," She smiled, before pressing her lips against mine, before pulling away quickly and getting back to the feeds. Even if she told me, why did I not believe her?

Elena's POV

I let out a little sigh as gathered all the feeds and passed a few to Ryan. Why did Zac have to be here? and I had lied to Ryan about there being nothing between Zac and I. Truth is, we use to go out, for a year and it was serious, well as serious as a 16 and 17 year old can be. I glanced at Ryan as we walked down the aisle towards the first horse. Whatever I do I can't let Ryan catch onto what really happened between Zac and I, hopefully Zac would just get his horse and go. But something in me told me otherwise, I could tell that this wasn't the last I saw of Zac.

→ Chapter twenty-two

Hey guys!I know I said no new chapters for a little while, but! Quinn [teachmehowtoequitate] on tumblr wrote these amazing few paragraphs and I thought I'd upload it as Chapter 22! :) I added a few things on at the end, but she's written basically all of it! So yeah! :DMost of you didn't really like the Zac POV on the last chapter and to be honest neither did I :P So it won't happen again! Just thought I'd let you know :)Anyway, GO READDD-Bronxxp.s external link over there > is her tumblr. Go follow her.If you ever want to write something for TPB don't be scared to! I'd love to read it, and most likely I'll put it up here as a chapter, unless it doesn't go with the story line :) You can send it to me on my email: crzysndy@gmail.commy tumblr: showjumperx.tumblr.com - you'll have to fan letter it or message me on wattpad!!!

———

The tension in the air was unmistakable as Ryan and I finished feeding the last of the horses. As I shut the stall behind me I saw that Ryan, Allan and Zac were standing around a tall chestnut at the end of the aisle way, walking closer I realized they were discussing the upcoming North American Tournament at Spruce Meadows.

"John is having me drive them the horses, I'll be leaving the farm on Thursday" beamed Zac

"Well we will see you there," Alan replied. Casually I walked up to Ryan and he immediately put him arm around my waist. Zac turned his attention away from the chestnut he was holding

"So Elena, I hear that you're going to be doing the Encana Cup!"

"You heard correct" I replied quickly.

"That's so awesome, super proud of you! Maybe I could take you out for dinner to celebrate after you win!' he smiled.

Ryan tensed beside me "Yee-aah" I managed to stutter out "Just gotta see what's going on with other horses and stuff" he winked at me and I shot him a half hearted smile.

"Well I better hit the road; don't wanna keep the boss waiting! Nice seeing you Elena, Alan, Ryan" Thank god, I thought as he lead the chestnut onto his trailer and started driving down the long drive.

"Nice guy" Alan mumbled before turning on his Parlanti heel and heading back into the barn. Ryan removed his arm off my waist and turned to me face me "You promise, he means nothing to you?" his hazel eyes were full of concern mixed with a little bit of jealously.

"Ryan, I promise, he's just a friend" andbefore he could reply I stood up on my tippy toes and placed my lips on his.

———

"Flight 125, Louisville Kentucky to Calgary Alberta, you are now boarding."

The airport was relatively quiet this early in the morning, though the people who were there gave the 4 of us and a few other riders that where with us awfully weird looks. We were all wearing our white breeches, show shirts, and Parlanti's. Alan had decided it would be easier for us to leave for Calgary early on Monday rather than late Sunday night. When we got there Matt, Ryan and I would all be showing horses in various classes ranging from the 1.10m's to the 1.40m's.

"That's us" Allan announced and we all followed, Ryan and I hand in hand and Matt beside his dad.

"You excited?" Ryan whispered into my hair, sending tingles down my spine.

"Nervous" I whispered back. It was true, I was very nervous. I, Elena Moore would be showing at the biggest and most prestigious show venue in North America. Some of the best in the sport were registered in most of the classes I'd be competing in, some of which I've looked up to ever since I started riding. Richard Spooner, Ashlee Bond, Kent Farrington, Tiffany Foster, all of whom have way more experience than I do on the international level.

"Don't be, you are gonna kick some ass" he whispered back

"I hope so.."

———

The horses made it safe and sound to Calgary and we got to the show grounds they were already resting in their stalls, waiting for the first class of the day, which would probably be the easiest of the whole show, the 1.10m class. All in all the Peirce barn would have 20 horses competing this week, I, myself was riding 4 or 5 of them, but Maddie will be my main ride, she's the one I'll be competing on in the Encana Cup. This could be my big break in the international ring, I need to be focus 100% when I go into that ring.

→ Chapter twenty-three

Hello!

Well it's been a longgg time since I've uploaded and I'm so sorry!!!

Again this chapter was written by Quinn! I don't know what I'd do without her C: I haven't had any idea what to write for a while but gah she's amazing! She's on tumblr and you should all follow her! LINK OVER THEREE -->

Anyway, I have a feeling a lot of people will like this chapter! NOW GO READD!

- Bron

xx

Our first day at Spruce was exhausting. The horse I showed in the 1.20m's had turned out to be quite fresh after the long trip from Kentucky. After he tried bucking me off in the warm-up multiple times he refused twice in the ring resulting in elimination.

"I'm not going to blame you here Elena, he was obviously quite excited today but I'll take him in a few 1.10m classes tomorrow and Wednesday and you can try him in the 20's again on Thursday."

"Okay Alan, thanks" I tipped my First Lady down and stared at the ground as I made my way over to the North American Ring where Ryan would be showing a Sales Horse in the 1.30m's. Walking up behind the bay I placed my hand on his bum then on Ryan's leg, he looked down and smiled

"Just in time for the big show," he smirked then realizing my expression his turned to concern "What's wrong?"

"Oh just that naughty chestnut stopped twice and I got eliminated in the 10's, the 10's!" I sighed

"Oh El, that's really shitty, sorry to hear that," he placed his hand on top of mine and gave me a sincere smile.

"Don't worry about it," I said returning it

"Ryan, you're in," the gate person interrupted

"Good luck," I said as he walked the bay into the grass ring.

As I made my way to the rail to watch I looked to my left to see Kent Farrington standing there as well. Intriguing, maybe he's interested in the horse?

Of course Ryan's round was flawless. The horse jumped amazingly and Ryan easily steered him around the course.

"And that ladies and gentleman was our fastest trip of the class! Ryan Pierce is now Leading!!" the announcers at Spruce were so into their jobs, it was a welcome change compared to all the dull announcers back in America.

"That was great Ry!!" I exclaimed as I slipped the bay a treat.

"Ryan?" a voice behind me called, turning around I realized it was Kent.

"Hey Kent, what's up?" Ryan replied

"I like this guy, I think he'd be a great horse for one of my clients to move up to the 30's on. Mind if we come and try him tomorrow?"

Ha I knew it! I thought to myself

"That would be great! Just go talk to my dad, he deals with that sorta stuff"

'Absolutely, thanks Ryan' and with that he turned on his heel and walked the other way to most likely find Alan.

"Sweet! Think we just sold this horse!" Ryan exclaimed as he gave the bay, who seemed to very pleased with himself, a hearty pat.

Once everything was finished we finally made it back to the hotel at 9pm. Ryan and Matt were sharing a room while Alan and I had our own rooms.

"Feel free to order any food you want Elena, but you have to be ready to leave at 6am sharp,"

"Thanks Alan, thanks for everything" I gave him a big smile and slid the room key into the door, it beeped and clicked and I stepped into the large room.

"Wow all this to myself?" I breathed. The bed was huge and there was a mountain of pillows on top of it and even some chocolates placed on top of the sheets! Directly in front of the bed was a large flat screen on a dresser and to the left of that was a beautiful mahogany desk.

"Luxury!" I squealed before launching myself on the fluffy bed.

After a warm bath and a delicious dinner I pulled some PJ's on and opened up my laptop. Wow 27 new e-mails? I should check this thing more often! An e-mail from my parents:

Elena,

We hope you have a successful trip to Spruce Meadows. Whatever happens we love you and are ever so proud of what you have always achieved. We will be watching you live on TV while you ride in the Encana Cup!

Best of luck,

Love

Mom+Dad

Oh geez, they are seriously the best. Another e-mail from my best friend Sarah:

ELENA!!

When were you going to tell me that you and Ryan are dating?! Or that you're at SPRUCE MEADOWS right now?! Do I have to rely on the internet to tell me everything about my best friend? Geez!

You're famous though!! Check out this article I found about you!!

Hope to hear from you soon,

~S

Hmm people are writing articles about me?! Better see what this is about...

YOUNG RIDER ELENA MOORE LOOKING TO MAKE A SPLASH IN THE INTERNATIONAL RING, CAN SHE DO IT?

We all heard about the new no-name working student that the Peirce family brought onto their team. After a few somewhat successful local shows, we now find out that Elena Moore has made the trip to the Spruce Meadows along with her new boyfriend Ryan Pierce, Matt Peirce, and their father Allan. We also learn that she is registered for her first International Event, the Encana Cup! Will she crash and burn? Or will she rise to the occasion. Find out this Thursday as we talk about all the action at Spruce Meadows.

~A Circuit Gossip

What the hell?! Who is writing this stuff about me?? Crash and burn? Horrible images of Maddie taking a long and crashing through jumps flash in my head. No no,, no, I can't let these people get to me. I quickly shut my laptop and toss it back into my suitcase. Curling up into a small ball I try to make the awful thoughts go away. Then there's a soft knock at my door. Tentatively I unravel myself and make my way over to the door; I looked through the peephole to see Ryan standing outside. Quietly I opened it

"Hey" he said

"Hi" I replied

"Can I come in?" he asked

"Yeah sure," I opened the door all the way and he walked in. God how can someone look so hot in sweats and a t-shirt? Only Ryan can pull that look off. Brushing past him I plopped on my bed and sat cross legged.

"What's up?" I asked as he gently sat on the corner of my bed.

"I've just been thinking lately, just how much I've changed since I met you. Your just so much different then all those other girls I've dated, they meant nothing to me. When that guy came to our place the other day, I was just so, so jealous. But that made me realize how much I don't want to lose you. I love you Elena and I hope you feel the same about me"

Oh. My. God. The look on his face, how sincere he just was, he loves me? All my emotions overcame me and I burst into tears.

"Elena? shit, what's wrong? Was it something I said?" He asked moving closer to me,

"No, god no Ryan. I love you too, your perfect and you're so good to me. It's just I am so god damn nervous for Thursday. There's people writing articles about me and how I'm going to crash and burn in the International Ring and how I'm nobody. It's just frustrating because I wanna be somebody but everyone's so goddamn discriminating" I fell into his shoulder sobbing. He wrapped his arms around me and held me close.

"Elena, you are so talented. You and Maddie are perfect together; you're the only one who can ride that horse properly. Don't listen to what anyone says except for my dad. He wouldn't have put you in this situation if he didn't think you were ready. We all believe you can do it, me, Matt, Dad, your parents, Sarah, all the grooms, and all our clients. Everyone is here for you and we just want you to succeed,"

Pulling away from his shoulder I looked into his hazel eyes. God I love this boy, more than anyone knows. I planted a soft kiss on his lips.

"I love you Ryan Peirce. You mean the world to me and what you just said made me feel so much better. But please, stay with me tonight? I don't want to be alone, not right now" Gently he brought his thumbs underneath my eyes and wiped away my tears.

"I would love nothing more." After setting the alarm we crawled into bed and he wrapped his strong arms around me. That moment was so serene and I felt so peaceful, so safe.

→ Chapter twenty-four

_____ "Don't you worry don't you worry child, see heaven's got a plan for you," I gently sang the words to the popular Swedish Mafia song to Maddie as I braided her gray mane. It was around noon on Thursday, the Encana Cup would be starting at 3:00 and I was 13th out of 32 riders, lucky number 13. I'd isolated myself from everyone, putting Maddie in the last crosstie in our row of stalls then I'd plugged in to my phone. So far I'd only run into a few of our grooms and I'd like to keep it that way until I had to start warming up. Maddie was content to have me working on her, gently leaning to one side she was dozing, her lower lip drooping. My large jumper buttons were all perfectly lined up, and I only had a few more, but I'd been braiding for a while so I decided to take a break.

"Such a good mare," I gave her a hearty pat on her muscular shoulder as I stepped off my stool. It was relatively hot out and so I decided to go in search of water. Quietly I tip toed to the front of the crosstie and peered out into the aisle way, some of the horses turned to look at me but other than that, coast clear. With James Bond like stealth I shuffled to the tack room and ducked in the corner where the mini fridge was, very carefully I pried it open, grabbed a bottle of water and turned around only to walk right into...

"Matt, hey," I stammered looking up at him

"Elena. Ryan's been looking for you everywhere!" he exclaimed

"I've kind of been hiding, need to get into the zone,"

"I see, well I won't tell him I saw you then." he winked down at me before letting me pass. I made my way back down the aisle to where Maddie was still dozing. As I stepped back onto my stool Matt appeared at her head. She perked up as he slipped her a carrot and ruffled her forelock.

"You do know we have grooms for that kind of stuff right?" He grinned

"Of course, but braiding always calms me down," I said returning to the tedious task.

"Whatcha listening to?" he gestured to my phone.

"Just some indie music, the Black Keys I doubt you've heard of them"

"I absolutely love their album El Camino! Their music is brilliant" I turned to face him

"Seriously?! You have good taste in music, unlike your brother" I smiled

"You should check out this band out of Vancouver, they're called City and Colour, I think you might like their music. It's what I listen to before big classes," he gave me that genuine Matt smile, that smile that says he actually really cares about what you're talking about. Not the half ass smile that Ryan gives me most of the time.

"Thanks Matt, I defiantly will check them out"

"Well I'll leave you too it" he gave me that smile, again "Ryan goes before you and I go after you so we'll all warm up together. See you in a few hours for the walk!" and with that he turned on his Parlanti heel and left me alone again.

"God these Peirce brothers Maddie, so goddamn confusing,"

———————

At 2:00 sharp I was outside the clock tower at the International Ring waiting for the 3 Peirce's so we could walk to course. The gate person had already given me a map and it looked somewhat complex. The open water was involved as well as a number of skinny jumps, which Maddie was not a huge fan of. She's better suited to rocking back on her haunches and soaring over oxers, not pinging for upright verticals because she gets lazy with her front end over them.

"Excuse me," I turned my head to see a tall brunette lady wearing a sharp navy blue suit. She carried a voice recorder and notepad in her left hand and offered me her right hand.

"My name is Jamie Tolright, I'm with the International Ring magazine. Your Elena Moore, correct?"

"That's me" I grasped her hand and shook it.

"I was wondering if I could ask you a few quick questions?" she asked

"Of course" I gave her a tight smile. Alan had prepped me for this, be calm and cool and give to the point, honest answers.

"There's a lot of experienced riders in today's field, what advantages do you think you have over them?" she'd started recording and had her pen poised on her notepad.

"I think I have a brave and honest horse, she tries her heart out every time we go in the ring. I've also had fantastic coaching over the past few months and I believe I am as ready as I will ever be for this class" that was to the point right? She eagerly wrote down a few notes before glancing back up and firing another question

"What do you think of Alan Peirce as a coach?"

"Alan is an amazing teacher. He has a wealth of knowledge and experience when it comes to shaping people into amazing riders. I have learned more from riding with him in the past few months than I have since I started riding" Alan should be happy with that one, promoting his training.

"It's been speculated that you and Alan's son, Ryan, are more than just friends. Care to elaborate?"

"Erhm excuse me?"

"That's enough Jamie" turning around Alan was behind me with a stern look on his face.

"Thank you Elena, that will be all," Jamie nodded at Alan before turning on her heel and walking towards the warm up ring to bother someone else.

"Sorry for taking so long Elena, the 20"s went over time and I had a client in that class"

"Not a problem Alan," I smiled at his concerned face, he was such a fatherly figure to me and I loved that about him. Behind him Ryan

and Matt came around the corner in their matching white Animo
pants and show shirts. Ryan's face erupted into a massive smile when
he saw me. Alan and Matt walked underneath the clock tower leaving
Ryan and I alone for a second.

"Hey," he grinned resting his forehead on mine.

"Hey," I breathed before he placed a gentle kiss on my lips.

"Where you been all day?" he asked pulling away and grabbing my
hand

"Around," I grinned.

———————

"Matt you'll get around 6 here depending on the pace your going,
Elena seven no questions asked, and Ryan 6 as well" Alan had been
giving us all our striding as we went around the winding course. I'd
taken a chance to look around at the other riders walking the course;
some of the greats were in this class. Richard Spooner, aka the Master
of Faster, Rich Fellers named USEF Rider of the Year last year, Eric
Lamaze, reigning Olympic Gold medalist, his students Tiffany Foster
and Caitlin Ziegler, McLain Ward, Leslie Howard, Brianne Goutal,
Ashlee Bond the list went on. The last jump on course was one of
Maddie's worst enemies, the skinny bicycle vertical measuring at least
1.50m, it was easily the hardest jump on course.

"Elena LOTS of leg to this one, ride her really uphill and squeeze
on landing. The time doesn't stop until you go through the finish
line so gallop the last few strides,"

"Got it," I tried to make myself seem like I was in the moment and
paying attention, but I really wasn't. My stomach had been churning

this whole course walk. What am I doing here? Registered for this class. There was no way I could pull off a clear round; some of these distances were wacky, set on half strides. This course was the hardest thing I've ever had to tackle and right now I wanted to be a million miles away.

———————

I flattened the crisp white pad on Maddie's gray back. The Pierce training logo looked sharp against the brand new white fabric. On top of that I placed my white Olgilvy pad and finally my Antares close contact. Maddie could sense something was up, maybe it was my mood or the special equipment she was wearing, other than the new saddle pad she had brand new leather Antares open fronts and hanging on the bridle hook was an absolutely stunning Antares figure eight bridle. Everything matched my saddle and everything made Maddie look like a million bucks. The boots had been a gift from Alan and the bridle was a gift from Ryan. I'd told both of them I could accept neither but they wouldn't take no for answer, combined I knew both gifts were well over $1"000 but they refused to take them back.

20 minutes later I was seated on Maddie. We'd been walking for a while when Ryan strutted in on his mount Voyager. The tall black gelding looked superb, like he'd stepped straight out of a fairytale. Ryan looked dashing in his Animo show clothes and polished show Parlanti's. Behind him Matt was on his horse for the class, Apollo who was actually Maddie's full brother. They look almost identical excepted Apollo's mane and tail were a shade darker. Matt was

sponsored by CWD so Apollo was decked out in CWD open fronts, breastplate, bridle, and saddle as well as the Peirce saddle pad but with the CWD logo on it. They both smiled at me and made their way onto the rail with the other riders. Tiffany was first in for the class so she was already popping Victor over warm up jumps. I noticed Eric was in the center of the ring setting jumps for her, when she went down the long side he snuck a quick glance at Maddie and I. Eric Lamaze. Looking at me? Seriously?! Quickly he turned his attention back to Tiffany. Focus Elena.

I asked Maddie to pick up a trot, she swished her thick gray tail and obliged. She was extra soft in the bridle today and seemed to be pointing her toes more than usual. What a little show off! She knows what's going on! I gave her a quick scratch on the withers then asked her to shorten then extend. We changed direction and trotted a few more laps before I asked for her canter. She seemed to be floating today, she felt so smooth, a million times better than normal. Just to make sure I wasn't imagining things I asked her to shorten, immediately she shortened her stride, then I asked her to lengthen again an immediate reaction. We did a flying change and did the same thing the other way. She felt balanced both directions and she was responding perfectly. Asking her for a walk I gave her a big pat

"Good girl!" I praised

"My crew over here" Alan gestured to the far left jump, all of us had warmed up our horses and were ready to pop some jumps. I'd noticed Matt's horse giving him a little bit of trouble, snaking his head and crow hopping but it was nothing he couldn't handle. Matt was the best rider out of all of us, quiet and patient but yet he could flip a switch and make his horse really fly when they needed too.

"Elena, Maddie looks superb. Whatever your doing is defiantly working so don't change a thing! Go pop this then I'll make it an oxer, then raise it and go from there" picking up my reins we did a perfect walk to canter transition then I pointed her at the vertical.

"One, two, one, two, one, two" silently I counted down and then let Maddie jump up to me, I sunk into my heels and we sailed over the vertical. All 3 of us did Alan's usual warm up routine, vertical, oxer, raise, vertical, oxer, raise and then go into the ring, Ryan was the first to go.

"Good luck" I said as I halted Maddie beside Voyager.

"Thanks Elena" he smiled then turned on his game face. Voyager cautiously stepped underneath the clock tower then onto the brilliant green grass. I heard some girls scream; Ryan and Matt had a very large and loyal fan base. Then I tuned out, and waited. I didn't want to watch any part of his round, me just being overly superstitious. I just wanted to go out and do my own round and have it go the way I want it to go, I don't care if I get time faults I just want to get around with no rails.

"And now ladies and gentlemen, we welcome Ryan Pierce to the Encana Cup today Ryan is mounted on Voyager" the speakers boomed and following that was the clang of the bell. Focus Elena, Ryan's on his own now.

Maddie and I walked around the area near the clock tower, people were running everywhere, trainers, riders, grooms, jump crew, camera men, it was really a big kafuffle. But Maddie was cool as a cucumber, Alan had told me that in Europe she had started showing at a very young age, so nothing really fazed her. The crowd that filled the grandstands in the International Ring groaned, I turned to look at Matt across the ring and he shrugged.

"Ryan leaves the ring today with 4 faults putting him in 5th place out of the 12 rides today" From underneath the clock tower Alan strode out and motioned for me to come over. He placed his hand on my white Tailored's and looked up at me with a smile on his face.

"Now Elena, just keep calm. The clock doesn't matter just get around the course and keep the jumps up. Keep a steady pace down the lines and let Maddie do her own thing with the oxers. Remember to ride her uphill with the skinnies. I'm so proud of what you have achieved with this mare, and the rider you've become. Now go out there and do what you are meant to do" tears brimmed in my eyes.

"Thank you so much Alan, I'll make you proud" and with that all the fear and emotion subsided. I knew what I had to do and the adrenaline pumped through my veins. Alan patted Maddie on her bum as we walked underneath the famous clock tower for the first time. Maddie calmly walked down the small hill and into the ring. I took a glance around there were people everywhere, I could hear camera's clicking and hushed voices.

"WOOO GO ELENA!! WE LOVE YOU!" I turned to see where the voices were coming from, two little girls were jumping up and down they stopped when I glanced at them and started frantically waving

"YOU CAN DO IT ELENA!!" they started jumping up and down again and I shot them a big smile. Focusing my attention back to the task at hand, Ryan and Voyager walked past us, he mouthed the words:

"Good Luck, I love you"

I mouthed back

"I love you too" and with that I asked Maddie to pick up a trot.

"And now ladies and gentlemen we welcome Elena Moore to the Encana Cup, she is riding Take Flight"

We headed directly to the hut in the middle of the ring, which held the sponsors in this case the people from Encana. I halted in front of them, stuck my right hand out and dipped my First Lady in a salute. The man stood up, took this cowboy hat off and clanged the bell. Picking my reins back up we cantered away from the hut and towards the first jump. In total there were 12 efforts on course, the first being a large inviting green oxer. We turned onto its track and Maddie pricked her ears. Silently I counted the strides until the fence and we easily found the perfect take off spot. Maddie rocked back on her haunches and soared over the oxer, she gave a big kick in the air as we landed and swished her thick tail. We landed and I counted 8 strides to the next jump, a blue wall which she glided over with ease. The next effort was a combination, a vertical then two strides to an oxer but it was a long two strides. Maddie's pace was kind of lacking, so I asked her to lengthen a little bit.

"Sorry Alan but I need to think for myself here" I muttered. We approached the vertical and I realized we were going to chip really bad,

I gave her a sharp half halt on my outside rein and she slowed down, we found the distance and she jumped the first vertical perfectly. I squeezed with my calves as we landed and Maddie burst forward

"Whooaahh Mads!" but it was already too late, we'd missed the optimum take off spot and Maddie took off too close to the base of the oxer. I squeezed as she took off and prayed, prayed that it would stay up. Her front legs gave the pole a good rub and I thought for sure it was coming down. As we started our descent back to the ground she kicked out with her hind feet to make sure we didn't hit it again. We landed and I waited for the thud, but it never came. Ignore it Moore, keep riding. The next jump was a natural looking oxer, which we cleared, and then it was a rollback to a vertical then a flat gallop to clear the open water. We'd schooled the water at home but Maddie wasn't a big fan of it. She slowed a bit as it came into her view but I gave her a little spur and she surged forward. I flattened myself on her and she spread over the water, there was no splash but there was no time to think about that, in 7 strides we would be going into a tight triple combination. I sat back and half halted she reluctantly slowed we got up over the first jump and I half halted on landing, over the second and she gave it a slight rub with her belly and finally the third, upon takeoff I gave her a little spur and she was nowhere near the rail.

"Good mare!" I sang as we galloped onto the next obstacle, an oxer with rainbow colored poles with large butterfly standards. This was the widest oxer on course, 1.60m in width but Maddie had no problem with it, she must've cleared it by 2 feet! The next 2 jumps breezed by and then we found ourselves going down the last line on the course. Between Maddie's ears I could see the bicycle skinny at the end and then the finish line but in fronts of us was another upright vertical. The thought of the clock flashed through my mind, and I realized we were going pretty fast. I also realized the crowd was dead quiet; the only sound was Maddie's hooves pounding over the grass. The vertical was upon us and Maddie launched herself over it and I remembered Alan saying "Elena seven, no questions asked" so I sat back, half halted and squeezed riding Maddie uphill to the skinny. She started sucking back so I gave her a little spur and she went forward.

"Four, five, six, seven" I let Maddie jump up to me and she did her signature kick and tail swish, when we landed I spurred her and we galloped across the finish line. The whole crowd who had been on the edge of their seats, erupted into cheers. Maddie broke to a trot and with complete awe I looked around the stadium, everyone was on their feet cheering and applauding Maddie and I. My face broke into a massive smile and tears started falling down my face.

"We did it Mads, we did it!" I gave her the biggest pat because she deserved it because she was the best horse. She'd carried me around this difficult course and had barley questioned me. I looked up to check the clock and realized we were well under the time allowed. By this time Maddie had slowed to a walk and we were walking to the clock tower. Alan and Ryan were standing next to Matt who was mounted on Apollo waiting to hear the verdict.

"And that ladies and gentleman was a clear round and our fastest of the day! Putting Elena Moore and Take Flight into first place!"

Alan leapt into the air and grabbed Ryan in a massive hug; my hand flew to my mouth in shock as I gasped. FIRST PLACE!! Matt walked Apollo under the tower and towards me, he held up his hand and I high fived it

"Now how am I supposed to ride after that?!"

"Shut it Matt, go kick some ass" I laughed as he trotted Apollo away. Maddie and I walked underneath the clock tower and before I knew what was happening I was pulled off of her and into Ryan's arms

"That was so amazing Elena, absolutely perfect!!" he exclaimed over my shoulder

"Ryan, you're crushing me!" I squeaked

"Oh geez sorry" he broke away from me with the biggest smile on his face. I felt someone's hand on my shoulder.

"That was brilliant Elena, I am so proud of you" I was swept into another massive Peirce hug, this time from Alan.

"Thank you Alan, for everything! I wouldn't have just done that if it wasn't for you and all you've done for me to make this possible. I hope to have many more rounds like that in the International Ring" he pulled away from me and I noticed he had tears in his eyes, then he turned on his Parlanti heel and walked the other way before I could say anything.

"Hey, let's watch Matt ride!" Ryan grabbed my shoulder and turned me to the gate

"But Maddie.." I protested

"Don't worry one of our grooms is walking her, come on!"

———

A few hours later I was seated on my tack box in front of Maddie's stall. She was contently munching on her hay after being pampered by the grooms for her performance today. After all the dust had settled we'd placed second, right behind Matt and Apollo. There was a massive blue rosette hanging on Maddie's stall and we'd also received a cooler. My phone hadn't shut up for the past few hours, calls and texts from all my friends and family as word had spread about my success in the International Ring. I'd been part of a press conference after the class had ended, Matt and I had been asked lots of questions but the one that I couldn't answer was "So Elena, where do you go from here" and to be honest I had no clue. This was my last month with the Peirce barn as one of their riders. My round in the Encana Cup could've been my last ride ever on Maddie. And Ryan and I? Will I go back home? Will another rider want me on their team? All these questions I couldn't answer...

Footsteps coming down the aisle made me look up.

"Elena I was hoping to find you" Alan sat down on Matt's tack box on the other side of the aisle.

"Your ride today was absolutely brilliant; I think you already know that. You also know that your time with us has come to an end and Ryan and Matt are quiet upset about that, which is why I'm here with a proposition for you. We would like to extend you an offer to be a permanent rider on the Peirce team, you will continue riding Maddie as well as your regular horses back at home but we've recently acquired some young prospects from Europe and we will need someone to help us with them we would also like to give you the opportunity to further your presence in the International Ring, you will come with us to Europe next month, but only if you accept" a large smile spread across his normally stern face. A permanent position on Team Peirce? Young European horses that they need my help with? Go to Europe and compete over there?

"Of course Alan, thank you so much for this amazing offer and everything you've done for me. It would be an honor to have a permanent position on Team Peirce!" as I finished my sentence Maddie stuck her nose out of her stall and prodded me in the back with it.

"Well it looks like Maddie is happy about that!" he chuckled.

CPSIA information can be obtained
at www.ICGtesting.com
Printed in the USA
LVHW080550280223
740519LV00015B/266